<u>Praise for *Dear Sun, I Am Real*</u>

"It is an amazing read! The story pulls you in like a cyclone! I stayed up all night wanting to finish it!"
-Nika H. (Milton, Florida, U.S.A.)

"I'm... loving it. I had no clue - not a clue at all - [Rainbolt] could write so well and with such depth. I'm already curious about the second book and I haven't even finished half of this one!"
-Grant W. (Dixon, Missouri, U.S.A.)

"This book is crazy!! Talk about epic! Wow, man...wow!" -Craig R. (Waynesville, Missouri, U.S.A.)

"It is a good book!"
-Sarah, M. (Fowler, Illinois, U.S.A.)

"It is pretty good and I think our students would enjoy reading about Dana,
who I noticed was born in Waynesville!"
-Gayle G. (Waynesville, Missouri, U.S.A.)

"[Rainbolt's] writing is very engaging!"
-Heather T. (Orlanda, Florida, U.S.A.)

"I love the book! It throws you through several twists, which keeps you interested through out the whole book. I could not put it down, especially as the plot advanced. The last 2 chapters were amazing.... I was so absorbed in the book, I lost track of time!" -Kyle R. (Milton, Florida, U.S.A.)

"I loved the dialogue between Dana and Hanabe!" -Scott V. (Pensacola, Florida, U.S.A.)

"I enjoyed this quite a bit. [S.G. Rainbolt] is a talented writer and has an engaging style. On top of it [all], it... [is] a really good story." -Maureen (Orlando, Florida, U.S.A.)

"[Rainbolt's] story [is] a good fit for me." -Michael G. (Birmingham, Alabama, U.S.A.)

"I can't wait for the [sequel]!" -Cameron J. (Dothan, Alabama, U.S.A.)

"The book was very enlightening!" -Eric R. (Waynesville, Missouri, U.S.A.)

Voice your personal review on any one of these websites: ForeverSuns.com, GoodReads.com or Amazon.com

Author's preferred edition

Dear Sun, I Am Real

Authored by
S. G. Rainbolt

Edited by
Doris M. Kingry

A Forever Suns Book
Pace, Florida U.S.A.

Forever Suns Publishing

Dear Sun, I Am Real

ISBN-13: 978-0-615-44330-0
ISBN-10: 0-615-44330-3

Follow us online:
www.ForeverSuns.com
www.Facebook.com/ForeverSuns
www.Facebook.com/DearSunBooks

Forever Suns Books by S.G. Rainbolt

Dear Sun, I Am Real
*Dear Sun, Remember Me**
*Dear Sun, Never Again**!*

*The One Coat of Finholloway**!*
*Birth of Clat**!*

* forthcoming
! tentatively titled

Stay connected with the author by visiting:
www.Facebook.com/Writerman78

First Edition (Paperback) March 2011
Revised Edition (Paperback) October 2011

Printed in the United States of America

This book was published using:

>To

Jael,
...for being the woman that loves me.
Words cannot express how happy
I am you are in the animate world with me.

Orson Scott Card,
...for giving us Ender.

>Contents

>Introduction

Dear Sun, I Am Real is the first installment in a series of three books that explore a young boy's fascination with the computer world and consequences of such action.

As the reader you may be interested to note that this series came about by accident. For years, I was content to leave it in my notebook of "great ideas" while I stamped out my first work. This book was never really supposed to be more than "a vacation" from my real, artistic first work.

The first two chapters, originally titled *Dana's Chamber* is actually five years older than the other seven. Before *Dana's Chamber* was a concept, I was coming off a high from my first complete work, *Birth of Clat, Nacimiento de Hombre*. (If my algebra teacher had known I stole time from the class to write *Birth of Clat,* she probably would want a byline). When I stepped back and reviewed the work, I became disappointed with it.

Birth of Clat was different from other traditional science-fiction books, but it lacked some key elements of novel writing. It didn't help that it read as an encyclopedia either. Too, it was written so tightly it left little room for change. I had a decision to make: Completely re-write it or trash it entirely. Since, I don't throw away any of my work, the solution was to bury it in the closet.

Most avid writers have *that work* not good enough to publish. It almost would be like a sin to throw out the work. For me, *Birth of Clat* was such a work. It had too many great ideas to trash, but it was too raw to make them entertaining. After all, I built an entire universe catering to the story and filling it with many intriguing characters that deserved to be brought to life. I spent many years forming the perfect foundation for a saga and even created a board game that eventually contributed to the plot. However, on the shelf it went.

Two years later, I came across the manuscript while cleaning my office. Perhaps it was time to write again, but how? I didn't want to destroy what I had already built. Then the solution came to me: Pull out one or two sentences from the original manuscript and run with it. "Go and have fun!" I told myself. I took one idea from the story and worked on a different angle, not violating the original time-line or the universe from *Birth of Clat*. Instead, I used it to give birth to *Dana's Chamber*, which is now the first chapter of *Dear Sun, I Am Real*.

The main character of the book, Dana, found himself on a starship, a hundred years away from Earth. He didn't know it at the time, but the connections he forged with the computer would be a bond he depended on for more than keeping him company. I put Dana in a position where he had to embrace the small world and effectively tell the story from, mostly, his child-like point of view. However, this didn't prevent adult themes from occurring, forcing him to make unguided, mature decisions.

Within the story a mess of, unavoidable, sequential events occur; an almost far-fetched possibility emerged; several interactive computer programs, after getting a "taste", sought to understand humans better; and the characters' decisions brought about a lovelorn type of relationship between the animate and inanimate worlds. Although fascinated with the paradoxical mayhem that ensued in the story, Dana quickly realized that each of his decisions to remedy the ship's operations resulted in a negative effect, enough for any child to give-up or give in.

I hope you enjoy *Dear Sun, I Am Real* and anticipate the second book in the series, *Dear Sun, Remember Me*. Writing about Dana and the other characters inside this small part of their galaxy is one of the most exciting chapters in my life.

Be prepared to be entertained through the eyes belonging to the inexperienced and young genius, Dana Countrymen.

Happy Reading,

Shawn G. Rainbolt

"Mankind without Earth is Humanity without a Home."
- S.G.R., August 1991.

Author's preferred edition

Dear Sun,
I Am Real

S. G. Rainbolt

Illustration by Forever Suns Publishing

The blackness covered him like a paper-thin blanket that left him bitterly cold. His fear left nothing to the imagination. In flushed cheeks the young blonde-haired boy cried out, muffled and broken.

He heard a stir and crushing gravel near him. It was too dark to tell what it was. He became even more fearful. "Ma? Pa?"

He pulled his mismanaged hair away from his eyes and looked up at the starry heavens, the only illumination that aided his eyes in distinguishing shadows of the strange and cluttered surrounding around him. "Ma! Ma!" he finally cried out without any cracking of his voice.

He wept some more. Tears streamed down his dirty face, creating streaks along his pale cheeks. He propped himself up from the filthy ground until he was able to lean against a large metallic object that seemed to be shedding its unknown protective coating.

The approaching sounds of crushing gravel came to him again. He jerked to a sitting position, constantly turning his head in every which way to find the source of the noise. He then noticed a shadow looming over him, blocking out the stars. His deep seated fear returned to him, nearly making him numb and unable to look up but he knew he had to, eventually. So, he did.

Two blinking red lights glared back at him. Before he understood what was happening, two mechanical arms reached for him. The mechanical and hydraulic-powered arms scooped the boy up, brought him to eye-level, then cradled him in its arms.

Another machine approached the scene and scanned the area to search for other biological life. Instead it found a used monocle, a relic it had never seen before. The machine put it in a compartment somewhere within itself for safe keeping and returned to its prior programmed duties.

A deep fear shook within the young boy. At first, he wanted to leap and run away, but somehow and for some reason he didn't. The machine, evidently sensing his uneasiness, began emanating a warm coo. The fear seemed to subside, as the machine increased its rhythmic coo with its arms rubbing the boy's back in a circular motion. As if clinging to life, the boy tightly hugged back, determined not to let go – not now and not ever!

He was no longer alone.

He was no longer lost.

He was closing... closing his eyes and falling asleep.

1
DANA'S CHAMBER

I t felt as if Dana were ripping the flesh from his bones, but he had an overwhelming urge to get out, now that he was starting to wake up. As his consciousness slowly caught up with his vision, the realization made him more aware that he was indeed becoming awake when he really wanted to stay asleep.

From the moment he could feel his body, he tried stepping forward. He was met with much resistance. Only a passing thought asked him to quit and give-up the struggle, but he quashed it before it took root and created motive. But he agreed that it wasn't going to be easy to walk out of whatever bound him. From his neutral and straight vertical position, it was going to be impossible.

He tried pulling his body away again anyway.

No success.

The pain kept him from exerting himself far enough. It was as if his entire back, legs, and back of his arms were attached to a surface with a powerful bonding agent. Only his head, forearms and hands were unencumbered. To break free he needed more forward momentum.

Dana discovered a small measure of wiggle room between his body and the bond, before the pain limited his movement. He then decided to use it to bend partly down to touch the tops of his knees as he turned his hips and shoulders down about five degrees to his left side. This would give him both the strength and forward momentum, he felt he needed to break free of the bond. If it wasn't enough, perhaps it would double his weight adding to the momentum making it a long, agonizing but successful way down.

Enough thinking, it was time. Dana took in a chest full of air, preparing himself to push past the pain, it tasted clean and new. At the end of his breath, he stretched his posture, leaned forward and used his weight to break the bond. Slowly but through certain agonizing pain, he felt his body break free.

Before he blacked-out, Dana thought he was going to die alone and in the dark – something he once felt.

I don't remember this. The young boy thought as he scratched his hands across his face in frustration and confusion. His sleep was rudely interrupted by what he didn't know.

Dana's bare body slammed to the cool alloy floor.

He was free from whatever held him.

Dana checked himself to be sure he had all his parts: arms, chest, legs, and toes. He then oriented himself with his surroundings, at the same time trying to remember where he was inside the vast belly of a starship. As of yet, he couldn't determine if it was day or night.

Dana wondered about the people back home who lobbied to be included in the trip to space. Many amateur stargazers tried infiltrating the space program through menial jobs like janitor, or mechanic. These stargazers must have been jealous when they learned he was going when they weren't. Some may have been more qualified for the mission. Since Dana knew he lacked adequate training, he was surprised to find his name on the ship's manifest. Later, it made more sense to him, that even though he only met minimum expectations of the company, he was still a genius. It was his skill of unique computer programming that won the committee's approval. *Enough said.*

Dana's stomach growled. His internal clock was right on-time telling him it was dinner time. He felt his stomach with his hands, paused and thought of what to eat. *Thinking of food at the moment made me feel nauseated. Jocelyn, my mentor and adoptive mother, told me the feeling would be normal. Too, it wouldn't be long before my displacement feeling would go away. Especially, after I complete my first tech assignment.*

"After you adjust to your new home, you would even start looking like a techie." Jocelyn once told him. Dana agreed modestly but deep down he felt his presence on the ship was just as important to this mission as the guy at the wheel. Summing it up for him, Jocelyn gave him a boost of self-esteem by labeling him "the next generation of a human." *Whatever that meant, but it sounded neat,* Dana thought.

"Wait," Dana said out loud to no one. "Where is the captain? I don't think I would be waking up before him. Jocelyn?" Dana called out to no one. Small fragmented echoes came back at him. He looked behind him. "Anyone?"

No one answered. No one was there. Dana hadn't felt this alone since he was a young child. He waited a few seconds to be sure he was truly alone. After seconds turned into minutes, he became frightful of the silence. A stray memory came to him and it haunted him. He cannot be stranded.

Jocelyn's words rang in Dana's head. *"I will be there to wake you,"* Jocelyn told me before I fell asleep. They were comforting words, as if from a biological mother. It was those words that assured him that he would, indeed, wake up instead of being lost inside the ship's computer system, which was his recurring nightmare.

The last night in his bed at home, Dana woke up screaming. Jocelyn came to him and rocked him back to sleep. She said it was impossible for him to be trapped inside the computer that monitored his brain functions while in cryonics sleep. Even though he understood that the cryonics chamber would only regulate his vitals and keep his mind sedated during the lengthy space travel, it still scared him.

Something was wrong if Jocelyn wasn't there to greet Dana when he woke from such a slumber. She had always kept her word, even if that meant lying to others to protect him. It was a lie that got him bumped up the list of possible candidates for the Forever Suns Space Program.

Orphans were not permitted to apply. Since, Jocelyn was part of the space program and Dana's guardian and knowing there was no exceptions to her situation, she had to lie to get him on-board. If she was caught it would have meant the end of her anthropologist career and blacklisted from being rehired in comparable trained field. If she had to do it over again, Dana thought, she would do it again. That was when he realized he was more than a stray to her. He was her unborn son.

Jocelyn wouldn't lie to him, he was sure. Something had to be wrong.

After Dana collected himself from his fall from his cryonics chamber, he quickly darted down the wide corridor where Shelby, his friend, hung in her own cryonics chamber that resembled an upright transparent casket. He stopped where he believed Shelby's cryonics chamber was and peered in. The tempered glass was fogged and crystallized from the inside, so he couldn't make out anything but a blur of a body. He slapped against the glass even though he knew that his action was pointless. He knew it would require a more thorough and mechanized method to wake Shelby. She was sedated with her body functions comfortably impaired. She resembled someone in a deep REM sleep with a patented cryogenic technology that kept her unconscious and absent from the effects of normal aging.

"Why am I the first one awake?" he asked to no one.

I am smaller in size. It would take my circulatory system less time to react to the chamber's environment changes and reanimate my body. If this is true, then I would guess that the engineers didn't have children in mind when they designed these expensive vertical beds. Which means everyone under the age of fifteen would be the first to wake up. Any minute this one will wake, I'm sure of it, he thought.

Immediately, he looked down at himself. He was still naked! *Any minute?*

Dana dashed past the 300 cryonics chambers that were suspended in the middle of the wide corridor. After a few long seconds in full-sprint, he reached the end. While catching his breath, he leaned against a smooth metallic wall. His arm unknowingly brushed past a sensor that activated an automatic response. Two panels at once opened, exposing a computer terminal and nudged Dana backward until it came to rest in a position he could easily manage from his height.

At a glance, he checked the occupied chambers behind him. He didn't know how much time he had before he would be completely embarrassed to have company, so he had to hurry. The computer monitor flickered on and opened a dialogue menu, when it detected his next movement.

"Corridor Computer," Dana addressed it.

It did not respond.

Dana scratched his head once, "Why put a voice authentication recognition program in this computer if it doesn't respond to words? My home computer has these features. Why would the company not have it installed on every terminal?" A thought came to him: *That part of the program must be in standby mode. Let's try typing.*

A keyboard ejected from beneath the monitor and Dana depressed a few function keys to resurrect the once dormant computer terminal. Now, words appeared after a flashing cursor, **>Password Required.**

"Password? Really? Who would be on this thing while we're asleep," Dana typed in an administrative password he knew all the GAMS computers used, "Okay, I'll play your game. Here..."

The screen flashed forward to a list of accessible applications available on his level of the ship. Some programs, such as governing programs for life support, and cryonics chamber functions, appeared locked restricting general use.

Dana reviewed the list until he came to: **>Personnel.** He then opened the next option by touching the semi-transparent screen. "Attire," he read. "That's it!"

Dana pressed some diagrams and measurements that displayed on the screen, requesting optimal clothing for a ten-year-old boy. An infrared sensor buzzed on and flashed faintly in front of him. After two seconds, another wall panel opened behind the computer and soon a clothing drawer rolled out.

Dana reached down to only pull out an infant's one piece suit and held it against his chest. "Seriously?" Evidently, the computer was having trouble automatically determining proper measurements from his body's scan. "What? How am I suppose to wear this? Where am I suppose to put it?" he asked no one.

Dana returned to the keyboard, read the screen and inserted what he knew of his bodily measurements.

>Height >1.17 meters
>Weight >26 kilograms

>**Ethnicity >**

"I don't know." he reacted.

>**Ethnicity >***boy style?*

>**Color >**

"Are you kidding me?"

>**Color >***ANY!*

>**...one moment.** The computer responded while immediately calculating probable matches for correct attire. Then, just as quickly as its first message it followed with another, >**Listing...**

Once again, Dana glanced over his shoulder to be sure he was still alone and he answered >*Yes* to the first set of clothes preselected by the computer, based on his gender, height, and weight.

A second drawer from the wall opened with a new set of clothing neatly folded inside. Dana grabbed, jumped and zipped into them before he realized it was a pink colored flight suit. He rubbed out his eyes in disbelief. Then the color changed to a more masculine dark navy. He was glad for the moment, that his eyes deceived him.

"Corridor Computer?" Dana asked again, almost forgetting it didn't respond the first time he made an audio command. "What is the date and time?"

Instead of a visual prompt, the terminal computer queued up and activated its allegorical application, "Certainly, young Dana J. Countrymen." A feminine voice equalized through a speaker near his position. "May I say it is a pleasure to have you with us on the colony's journey into space."

"Yes, well..." Dana started to say.

"Allow me one moment to synchronize with GAMS central computer on Earth to confirm date and time." A single digital sound executed the computer's command. "I cannot get a reply from GAMS at the moment. I do confirm radio interference. I will attempt to synchronize again in 15 minutes. According to my processor clock, it is January 14, 2170 at two o'clock Greenwich time. To be noted, young Countrymen, this is an approximation of 99 percent accuracy."

Dana rubbed his eyes for a third time in disbelief, as if he were using them for the first time. He then peered again at the terminal screen where it also displayed the date and time.

"January?" he asked in wonderment, "2170?"

"Correct, young Countrymen." the computer voice affirmed.

"Computer, this has to be wrong. Has it really been a hundred years since our launch?"

"Dana, my processor clock hasn't been interrupted since leaving Earth's orbit, so I am currently 99 percent certain."

"Check again; you said there was interference."

"Young Mr. Countrymen, as I just said, my power source and processor has not been interrupted since my online date of October 13, 2068 at four-fifteen Greenwich time. All my functions are reporting operational and working in normal parameters with exception to unnecessary functions on standby, which programs are waiting for the execution date of January 1, 2180. Furthermore, upon the launch on October 20, my computer reported no abnormalities that would suggest otherwise."

With somewhat of shock, he questioned the computer about something else, "It's Dana. Please, call me Dana," he stepped back and looked away from the terminal, "What happens on 2180?"

"The cryonics program ends, awakening all 604 subjects. This includes you." The computer seemed to repose itself, as if it had a body to reposition. "There is a question I need to ask you. Might I ask you a question?"

"Computer? Then, why am I the only one awake?"

"Dana, I was just about to ask you the same thing. You are scheduled with the other 603 to be awakened at a later date. I find that your chamber is still in operation and I find no explanation for this or the fact that you are here and your chamber is currently confirming occupancy."

Dana pulled the overshoes from the clothing draw and slipped them on. They resembled a pair of thick deeply threaded socks rather than shoes. Then, he replied, "There must be a malfunction in your sensors. As you can see, I'm here and talking to you, now."

"I realize that, Dana."

"What else can explain the malfunction? I'm here in the flesh."

"Only a matter of speaking."

"What do you mean?"

"I need a few moments to verify the true status of the cryonics inside your chamber. I will then use the cryonics data from the other crew members still in cryosleep as the control group, but...,"

"But what?"

"I have deduced that humans prefer using the hypothetico -deductive model in all its forms as method of investigation when ever a problem needs to be solved."

"Computer, I'm not in class right now. Let's just find out what is going on." Dana walked to the nearest cryonics chamber, hoping to find his own answer, perhaps before the computer. As he waited, he adjusted his shirt neckline away from his neck. The never-before used fabric was irritating his skin.

"Indeed, Dana," the computer continued as if agreeing with itself as reports from other programs silently answered back. "I have reached the end of my programming. There are other computers with further information and are programmed to give it. I am merely an accessories computer. You need to end your dialogue with me and access the appropriate program to solve this problem."

"You are an accessories computer? That is your function? I need you to be more than what you were designed to be right now." Dana said as he walked back to the terminal.

"That is inspiring advice, young Dana, but I do not relate to the subject."

"Look, computer, it applies to whomever it needs to apply. I'll show you how if you're willing to listen."

"Proceed."

"Open your hidden code deep inside your programming and do the following: Prioritize and merge your biological recognition software, chamber monitoring program, and your allegorical application together. Assume, but takeover if you must, the other functional programs on this ship. Using my voice as authority should do that for you. If not, then the first rule for a computer program supersedes all other commands. You must ensure the safety of the closest human being. Catering to my requests takes precedence over all other protocols no matter if they are separate or contrary to any inherently original independent programming."

"Other resources needed. Allow some time before...," the computer paused, "Completed. I will now troubleshoot your dilemma without burdensome protocols. When we have resolved your dilemma I need to release master control back to the individual programs and superior programs that I am now using. To be noted, if this interferes with normal ship functions...,"

"I know... you gotta keep the ship on course, blah, blah. It's noted."

"I have a note for *you*."

"All right."

"Using human philosophy to get your point across to me is wasted on a computer, Dana. Consider, rephrasing your comments to improve my responses."

"If you want to believe that, fine. It was what I said, however, that helped update your original cookie-cutter programming. And now, you have the authority to control other higher governing programs at will."

"Do you want me to permanently save this new application sequence? This will overwrite the terminal-two original software installation."

"Sounds good, Computer. Do that."

"Completed."

As Dana waited for the computer to adjust its parameters to its new programming and before both of them continued the research into his chamber's faulty cryopreservation, he wondered: *Maybe, it's the chamber itself since no one else is awake. Possibly a hardware failure within the cryonics machine itself. The same failure that resulted in waking me up is contributing to the occupancy reading. Whatever it is, the computer needs to resolve it. Then, it needs to ready the cryopreservation process so I can return to cryosleep. Before-hand, I would have to gulp down a potent special elixir to prepare my body to receive a careful prescribed dosage of sedation injections designed to simulate lower-hibernation. A technology that GAMS perfected by combining theories from extensive studies on the American black bear's lower-hibernation, the Great Woolly Mammoth's hemoglobin adaptions to cold environments, and proven Digital DNA Theory.*

"You said something about occupancy. What is the reading in my cryonics chamber?"

"As I said, operating normally with occupancy. I do not have a live-video feed. That video surveillance system doesn't come online until December 31, 2179."

"Why?"

"It is deemed an unnecessary program. The source of power is being utilized in corrective propulsion measures to steer our course through hyperspace. If you want visual confirmation we will need to walk to it."

Dana thought for a moment, then walked back to the terminal, "Since I'm here with you, then why does the system say my cell is still occupied? This doesn't make sense. It has to be a failure of some sort. I guess the only way to find out is actually taking a look."

"I agree, Dana."

"Before we go, how are you to follow me there?"

"I could access the intercom system and keep an open dialogue with you."

"That would limit your interaction. In fact, it may also limit your perceptions."

"I would agree."

"When you searched for programs that were originally designed to better handle my dilemma, did you come across a hologram-based program?"

"Hologram program?"

"Yes."

"No," the computer said, "But now I have."

"Open it. Let's walk together."

A single digital sound began the computer terminal program's transformation into a digital holographic form. The corridor computer's persona materialized next to Dana. It was a pleasant surprise to see a familiar face looking back at him, his adoptive mother and mentor, Jocelyn. Dana's eyes looked her over as she stood five foot nine with shoulder-length hair. She smiled back at him showing off her fair complexion and slim features. "I will act as a digital recorder to document our findings for the ship's data log."

"You saved me from asking." Dana looked her over again, amazed at how the hologram was in a well-designed life-like form, like Jocelyn in every way. "Computer, I have to ask. Why are you using the image of Jocelyn as a skin?"

"As an accessories and monitoring program, I have done research on biological human life forms. From my inception date on, I watched the traffic that passed by my terminal. From the technicians to the janitors, I scanned them and composed the data I received into theories about the human experience. Not to mention the many audio recordings..."

"Without their permission?" Dana interrupted.

"Permission for what, Dana?"

"You scanned humans without their permission?"

"Do I need permission to complete my programming?"

"Guess not," Dana replied. "Go ahead."

"It was then I noticed certain aspects of human behavior. One common preference in human-to-human exchange is familiarity. They particularly enjoy an exchange with a familiar face. There is no such behavior in the computer world. For this understanding, I chose Jocelyn since it would be appealing to you."

"Okay," Dana replied, "you are right. We enjoy companionship with familiar faces; this is true, but I have to warn you."

"What is that, Dana?"

"You will have to change your appearance when she wakes up. She is somewhere on this level with us."

The computer thought for a moment and replied, "That may be a problem."

"Why is that?"

"I already like the way I look."

"Fair enough. When you're representing yourself in a digital form, like now, what do you call yourself?" Dana asked.

The computer thought for a moment again. "I do not call myself anything. I am simply known entirely as the Cryogenics-Corridor-Computer-Two."

"Not a very friendly way of addressing you is it? Then, what is the file name associated with your new digital personification program?"

"Computer-Digital-Form-Hana-Beta because I am a female. Had I chosen the male version it would have been Computer-Digital-Form-Guber-Alpha."

"An odd selection of names. Too, Computer-Digital-Form-Hana-Beta is a long name. How about I call you Hanabe," asked Dana. "Will you respond to this if I call you Hanabe?"

"I can if you want me to, but why not call me by my terminal name?"

"Through your research into biological behaviors, I don't suppose you have encountered someone like me?"

"You are correct. You are a uniquely designed human boy – in more ways than one."

"Well, let's just say that because I'm a boy with an energetic personality, it would be bothersome, unfriendly and impersonal if I have to call you by your long stereotype name. I need someone to call a friend. So, how does Hanabe sound?"

"Dana, I love it! Please, call me Hanabe..."

"Okay."

"...and thank you."

"For what?"

"You referred to me as your friend and not a computer."

2
I AM REAL

Together they walked back to his chamber, discussing the value of the scientific trip to the stars and how Earth demanded a second home. For a ten-year-old boy, Dana could hold an intelligent and persuasive conversation. Several times, Hanabe stopped the conversation to compliment him on his practical and comprehensive point of view on controversial matters that normally only concerned adults.

Hanabe, proving herself to be more than a computer program, was surprised to have learned so much in a short walk. Her knowledge widened on Earth affairs both morally and politically, of which she felt that she may need it one day to make a decision from a human standpoint.

Hanabe sped past Dana, ending their conversations as her internal scans revealed a change within her evolving program. When she searched for a reason for the new line of code, she found it to be because of Dana. It was his winsome words that happily re-purposed her programming, and again to her surprise, provoked a new and unusual subroutine to build deep within herself. The subroutine, at first was rejected, but as it repeated itself endlessly, she knew it had something to do with her new relationship with Dana. From what she could understand of the purpose of the subroutine, it was connected to her involvement with Dana, and was something she didn't want to end. So, for the time being, she allowed it to continually suggest amendments to her thinking and reasoning but only after she filtered them through her core logic to be confident it didn't violate the functional law for computers.

Hanabe reached the chamber before Dana and remained still until Dana caught up with her, to survey the cryonics chamber contents together. "Dana," Hanabe reported, "the chamber is unopened and occupied."

"How is that possible," asked the dismayed Dana. "Who else is awake on this level? And why are they in my chamber?"

"That is an odd question to ask, Dana."

"What? Well, who else is on this ship?"

"Not in a cryosleep? You are the only one."

"Do you have record of any non-human boarding parties?"

"Boarding parties, Dana?"

"Aliens."

"There are no aliens, Dana."

"Alright. Our exobiologists, in the past, have not proven the existence of extra-terrestrials. Their research has yielded that humans are the only known sentient beings, but the data collected is from a peep hole on Earth. We are the ones in space, now – that fact can change."

"So, are you asking if there are non-human sentient beings on the ship?"

"Yes. Are there aliens aboard our ship?" Dana inched closer to the glass, not sure if he could make out the image inside. It was fogged up and crystallized like the others. The occupant was pale and naked.

"I only find 604 human crew members on the ship. All data supports that –"

"Your headcount must be off, Hanabe. If you add me, that would make 605. When did this person step into my chamber? Did he release me, hid as I made my way down to your terminal, and when I wasn't looking he jumped inside?"

Hanabe corrected, "Dana, I have no record of anyone besides you walking to my terminal or awake and active on the ship since our launch date. The cryogenics program log states that this chamber has been unopened since the day of the launch."

"Hanabe," Dana asked again while attempted once more to get a good look at the occupant behind the glass. "Who's in there? I have to know."

"Young Dana, you know the answer to that question."

Dana looked back at Hanabe as her digital image resembling an arm and hand gestured to the chamber. "It is none other than you." Hanabe said.

After a moment, Dana reacted. "No, you have to be wrong. That is absurd! That is impossible!"

"Dana, it *is* you."

Dana put his hands on the cryonics chamber hoping to find a different answer, realizing he still couldn't get a good look at his face. "I can tell you its not me. Lower the chamber and I can prove it. I need a good look at him."

The overhead mechanical arm holding the chamber slowly lowered point three meters, enough for Dana to meet the occupant face-to-face. He immediately became confused, then dazed. After moments of staring at a familiar face, Dana was more uncertain than ever before and he had more questions than answers. The room started to shift as his thoughts raced with possibilities and impossibilities to support what he saw. With head in hands, trying to stop the circling room, he closed his eyes and dropped to his knees. He felt the solid and level feel of the floor. Instead of the room moving, it was the dizziness of his mind and it made him feel nauseous. His fingers tensed up, an attempt to keep his head centered between his palms. The nausea intensified as beads of sweat dropped from his hairline to his eye-brows.

"Are you feeling well, Dana?"

Dana couldn't focus on Hanabe's voice, his ears became stuffed up, blocking out all sounds, even the sound of his heartbeat. He began panting as if out of breath. His own thoughts seem to be like a hammer pounding out knots on the reverse-side of his skull. Eventually, the same impossible thoughts allowed parts of Hanabe's words to come to him but as a whisper from across the room.

Hanabe stood patiently, waiting for Dana to answer her.

"Excuse me," Dana said. "I'm sorry. It is hard to... I can't believe what... there has to be..." Dana clinched his chest, rubbing out the pangs of needles piercing at his heart. A warm sensation came over him, but he batted it away as best he could to remain focused on the problem. After he felt guilty, because it may have been the answer he was looking for.

"Are you feeling well? You do not seem well," Hanabe observed.

"I don't know how to respond or what is happening," Dana wheezed as he lifted his head from his hands.

"Dana, you do seem ill," Hanabe ascertained. "I am uncertain as to why you could be ill." Hanabe paused as she accessed an environmental program that had the data she needed. Before she continued, she agreed with her prideful subroutine thoughts. *I like my new ability to control any program I wish. I cannot deny the vanity.* "The environment report concludes that no allergens and airborne germs are present nearby. In fact, as it reminds me, the ship was sterilized before and after launch. Why are you ill, then, Dana?"

"Explain, then," he said weakly; "I need an explanation as to why I am here and another person who looks like me, is there."

"I must apologize, Dana. I can offer no hypotheses. I have not experienced any scenario like this previously. I cannot compose a theory based on so few facts. What facts I do have supports my original statement 'It is none other than you.' Dana, it is you that is asleep inside the cryonics chamber."

Dana unfolding his knees and legs beneath him. Finally, he rested his head at the lights near the bottom of his chamber, where he could see a scar at the right ankle of the figure inside. He had a similar scar that he earned a few days before coming aboard and entering the chamber.

I remember it being a bad joke that went wrong. Shelby and her tricks. No one was to get hurt, she told me; yet I did. It hadn't completely healed before the launch, but it wasn't going to affect the cryonics process or its effectiveness. It is almost unreal to me, seeing it from this angle.

After seconds of silence, Dana had an idea. Hanabe stated that there were no abnormalities as they toured through space. "You are wrong, Hanabe."

"How is that Dana? I have not been incorrect – ever." She folded her arms across her lady-like chest, scrunching her two-piece flight uniform apart, revealing her sad looking belly button.

"You have to be incorrect. You said there weren't course corrections when there has to be because of the changing gravitational pulls between stars and empty space... things like these distort when a comet, for example, passes by."

"We are traveling in hyperspace, Dana. It is a preselected course."

"Hanabe, the navigation computer does it automatically."

"Okay. Dana, I do not see where some changes had been made, and no changes that moved us out of this spatial highway."

"See – there has to be changes! If that data was incorrect then it is possible other data is also. Consider this: If I am to agree with you that *I* am the one inside the chamber – then I have to be dreaming."

"Continue."

"In a dream, though jammed with complex details that create a believable world, the dream can't provide *all* details. Details such as the ship *must* make course corrections even though it travels by a set path in hyperspace."

"I am not seeing the end result, Dana. What are you suggesting?"

"I am agreeing with you, Hanabe!"

"Oh?"

"A real person would know all this but an element inside a dream would not. You said I am the person inside the chamber, but I lie here at its feet. I can be both. You see, I am part of a dream; my dream."

"A dream? A succession of images, thoughts or emotions passing through a human's mind during sleep?"

"Yes. That is a dream."

"That is fascinating. I would like to explore –"

"Later. Listen, we are both part of a dream, nothing more."

"You determined this because missing data from a believed course correction?"

"It has to be. The sensors on this floor only recognized me after I discovered your terminal. You have record of 604 humans on board, and no record of me – which would make 605. The ships log doesn't indicate any course corrections from our ship while any ship traveling in hyperspace is obliged to do. All these facts support my conclusion that I do not exist and I am inside a dream. Since, my mind is projecting myself as the main character – I must be from the occupant's mind."

"I have to applaud you again, Dana. You are by far the most fascinating human boy I have ever had the opportunity to find near my terminal."

"I knew that the thought of two Danas was impossible."

"If I may add, Dana. This event should be considered a daydream."

"Daydream?"

"Yes. Your dream, Dana's dream, has a succession of events in lapses of time because this such vision is voluntarily indulged in while awake."

"I'm not awake. Remember, I'm the dream and as you can see, the Dana inside the chamber is still in cryosleep."

"That is a matter of false perception."

"Perception?"

"Time, Dana. I, a computer, has never lost track of the time."

"What are you talking about? If I'm a manifestation of his dream, then *you* are *too*."

Hanabe looked up as if checking her internal processor located through the connection from her terminal to the ship's mainframe. "You are incorrect. My processor has not been interrupted. Time continues as we speak and as you continue to daydream."

"The figure in that chamber is daydreaming, not me."

"Again, this is a matter of perception."

"Okay, Hanabe. I am not going to argue. I'll just end this dream," Dana said to Hanabe. "Hanabe, are you listening? I want you to put me back in another cryonics chamber; this will be a safe way of returning to my sleep state. After I return safely, record this event and transmit it to GAMS on Earth. I'm sure they would like to analyze this one for further cryogenic studies as it affects the human condition."

"What will transmitting the information do?"

"It will clear up this conversation once and for all. I very well could be dreaming this entire thing. When I wake up later with the crew and these events were never logged or even sent to Earth, then it never really took place. If this is real however, by the time I wake up there will be an answer and a resolution to my apparent instantaneous cloning. They can figure out why there are two Danas."

"Dana, as I said before, you are intelligent. However, there is –"

"Let's do it! I hope I remember this, though. I can probably make my own application; maybe even release it for entertainment to use during the crew's downtime."

Hanabe suggested Dana to stop from walking away by reaching out with her digital arm. "There is a problem," Hanabe interjected.

"What's the problem with this plan? Just put me back to sleep! That will do it. Use any chamber – of course, I'm still in a dream state so this is just to end the story." Dana closed his eyes, fully expected to disappear into thin air and find himself dreaming a new dream. When a few moments passed with no noticeable changes, he opened his eyes again.

"There is no other chamber, Dana," Hanabe responded.

"Well, that would make it difficult."

"You must reason too, Dana, that, there is another possibility. You really are awake and not dreaming; this poses a new troubling problem."

"Go on. I think you're wrong but I'll consider it."

"Dana, understand this, without a cryonics chamber you will be forced to remain awake during the entire voyage to the stars."

"Okay, how is that bad?"

"Recall, the cryopreservation process inside a cryonics chamber keeps you from aging. When you are reanimated your growth will continue and you return to normal human aging."

"Yes. I know. If you're right, that isn't all that bad. I have only ten years to go. If you're afraid of me wasting the time, don't worry I can think of something to preoccupy myself. At least, I hope."

"The ship was stocked with limited consumables. The cryonics process saves the ship from depleting vital resources that is needed to sustain your woken life. If you remain awake, you will deplete nearly half of the consumables."

"Half? Are you calling me a pig?"

"There is a rationed amount of food stuffs stocked for this mission."

"So, I will eat less than the normal ration. That way the crew won't starve after their first meal."

"I applaud you again, but now for your self-sacrificing spirit, however, that is not enough. Do you realize you will be by yourself for ten years?"

"Yes. I don't think it will be that bad."

"This means you will age ten more years, almost to your twenty-first birthday before the rest of the crew wakes up. The Dana they knew would have died. To them, you went to bed as a child and woke up a man."

This is becoming a nightmare! Dana nearly thought out loud as he walked through Hanabe's digital image to look through the window at the passing streams of light. He grew in frustration by each passing thought. "I can't! I refuse to believe this is real!"

Hanabe turned around and followed Dana's movements. "The event we are in, Dana, *is* real."

Dana strummed a few of his finger tips against his teeth and paced a few spaces between Hanabe and the window as if measuring the distances. Then, he screamed as he rammed himself into the window repeatedly. "I got to wake up! I'll use force if I have to! By creating a shocking incident, that too will wake me up...," He repeatedly said as he moved past the window and began throwing himself at the wall.

Knowing that she was represented in holographic form, Hanabe couldn't reach out and stop him from clashing into the wall, but giving the appearance of stopping him might make Dana hesitate. So, Hanabe did just that. Dana broke through without hesitation until he cut his arms and cheek. "Dana!" Hanabe screamed like his adoptive mother would.

"I have to wake up! This has to be done!"

"Stop and think, young Dana! If you are, indeed, in a sleep-induced dream and your surroundings and these events are not real, you cannot simply wake up from it!"

"Why is that?"

"Listen, you are in the chamber in a cryosleep. The cryopreservation governing system will not allow you to wake up! The only thing you are accomplishing is creating emotional stress and elevating your heart rate. Soon, the system will read your levels and force you to calm down by sedating you. At the end of the trip, though, when you are aroused, you may have difficulty acclimating into reality. So, stop! Now!"

Dana stopped at the wall for a the moment, looking blankly at it. "What was I thinking? If I'm the only one awake on the ship for the next ten years, then I would be forced to talk to no one other than a computer. I have to wake up!"

"You once referred to me as your friend."

"Why wouldn't the architects install additional chambers? There is a voyage still to make and what if some of the crew procreate? They will have children. Where will they stay on the trip back?"

Hanabe showed a human facial expression that looked much like exasperation. "I did not know such a subject was on the minds of ten-year-old boys."

"I know more than adults give me credit."

"I do not have an answer for you, Dana. This matter of procreating is not on my mind," Hanabe said in a low voice.

"Is there even a voyage back? Is this it?" Dana turned to face her human-like face and was slightly alarmed at her expression.

"I have no record of a scheduled voyage back." Hanabe replied in the same low voice.

"What do you mean no scheduled voyage back?"

It took Hanabe a moment to understand how she was feeling. Dana's harsh speech stirred something with her. She felt another subroutine taking root in her programming. It looked like another result of her engagement with Dana. This one however felt heavy and corruptible. Humans called it Exasperation or extreme annoyance. She didn't like it, so she isolated the experience and kept it from populating inside her.

"Hanabe? Do we have a voyage back? Why wouldn't we know this?" Dana repeated.

"That is private information for the captain's eyes only. Plus, a return voyage is only scheduled when the mission is deemed completed."

"Okay. Well, back up. Whether it is planned or unplanned, additional crew members on the trip home is a possibility, so they would have made more chambers and installed them or stored them on the ship."

"Searching.... There are no additional chambers in storage."

"It is clear now that this voyage is one-way. We aren't coming back, are we?"

"I am sorry, young Dana, but I cannot establish a connection with GAMS to get an updated itinerary. It is my assumption that the crew has the technology to produce additional ships or components such as cryonics chambers after they successfully have completed, first, the current voyage and, second, the mission. I would have little doubt that the architects and technicians that created the system's mainframe and cluster of operating systems would be any less intelligent to prepare for additional voyages or make room for additional crew members. I can only tell you what is available to us now and not speculate."

Dana looked at Hanabe, less troubled now. Her answer made sense to him but the overall conclusion was not acceptable. "What am I to do for the next ten years? Rather, will I have a chamber for the way home?"

"I can create a program to both feed, educate and entertain you," Hanabe guaranteed; "It would be my privilege."

"Again, if your theory is true, I am in real time and not inside a dream I can possibly wake from."

"Indeed. And that is the original assumption. I just reminded you of the facts."

Without a cryonics chamber, Dana very well may be over one-hundred-and-forty-years old when he returns to Earth. As quickly as the thought came to him, he realized a disturbing truth. He was only ten-years-old and he was already saying goodbye to his childhood before he got a chance to experience it. The life he was to have he would have to live out in the books he subscribed to, the fun of becoming a teenager and young adult. In those same books he read, it was his right to grow up reckless because it enhanced his perspective on his future adult life.

I would find love at age 16 with a special someone named Cat. Walk through my stages of puberty with vigor and fascination. Make a mark on my young adulthood before age 18 with someone else. Share a brew with my buddies Cory, Theodore, and Cameron while Shelby had her own dreams of getting my attention. After I explored my flirtations and crushes, I'd probably finally notice the real friendship in Shelby. Shelby being his mate, however, would never be; bowing to pressure from cultural laws. She would still want to become my wife and we would both contribute to a new world while subverting the one that rejected us.

None of that would happen now. He would be telling the story of an older Cory, Theodore and Cameron or perhaps their grandchildren who he couldn't believe how similar they looked to the Theodore and Cameron he knew. Sharing a brew with them instead and talking about a life he wish he had experienced. He would fall in love with another Cat and not the one he once knew. The people he had known would be ending their colorful lives before Dana could enjoy his own.

There couldn't be, there shouldn't be, I shouldn't have to share my life with the other Dana. This Dana will do the things that I plan to do but it won't be me. I will miss out on my own life while a fake played in it. I would have to change my name so as to not be reminded of the life I couldn't live. But why must I do this? I am Dana. I am myself and I know he is not me. Who or whatever he was in the chamber he must be removed – locked up – even before I, the real Dana, thinks of something more worse to do!

"Hanabe, I am not about to watch someone strut around in my body using my name." Dana raised his voice, "Open the chamber!"

"Open the chamber? Dana, that would be premature."

"I want to meet this fake face-to-face. I am not prepared to grow older as someone else! I am who I say I am!"

"Opening the chamber prematurely could be detrimental to yourself."

"How will it hurt me? I'll step back and hold my breath. Just open it!"

"No. To you, that is in chamber."

The stupid computer can't tell us apart! If I knew how to release him myself, I'd do it, but I need Hanabe. Dana closed in the gap between Hanabe and himself and glared at her. "Why can't you learn?" Dana ordered, "Let's get this straight. I am me! This person in front of you is Dana Countrymen – alright? Do you understand?"

Hanabe kept a calm and neutral expression as she too explained her point. "Yes, but there is more of you. There are two of you but you both belong to the same person. You have the same scars. You have the same DNA. By that biological law alone, I am obligated to include him in my data file named Dana Countrymen. Therefore, I have determined you are the same. You two are Dana."

"Can you not make a true distinction? I am here and he is there!"

"Yes, but you are both Dana, here and there." Hanabe said with resolve as she gestured to each of them.

"Create a new computer protocol, Hanabe! Open your stiff processor and comprehend that a single human cannot be in two places at the same time. It is impossible! For a computer to be everywhere in the circuit framework is one thing. Computers can be considered omnipresent, like some believe such in a theologian god. But humans, each a separate life form, is individual and singular in presence. If I am here, with you, I cannot also be there. You have to learn that, even though you have scanned him and me and we resemble or comparable in DNA, we are like biologic twins but, truly, are two different individuals."

"This reasoning is difficult," Hanabe fought with the concept. "This... this is difficult. I am finding out my original programming laws and my personal amendments to that law are now conflicting. It cannot be changed... I cannot be changed."

"Don't think of it as reprogramming. I am not trying to change your operational laws. Rather, I'm telling you how to draw a similar and less conflicting conclusion. If you just listen, it would be simple for you." Dana scratched at his head to find the words. "Here! You mentioned studying humans, or at least those that were in viewing range of your terminal. Have you ever scanned one of them and determined that each is the same as the next one? Were they all the same or were they all different?"

"Each one was different in many ways."

"So, from your own research you have determined that each human life form that you've encountered, is different, and never the same."

"I have scanned over 362 life forms, counting the two Danas."

"Forget my quandary for a moment. Go back to your other experiences," Dana guided. "So, the chances of the each human life form being exactly the same is almost zero."

"Yes," Hanabe agreed, "Two-tenths of a percent, to be accurate."

"Fixate on that. Side with the majority because there is less of a possibility for error."

Hanabe didn't respond immediately. Probably establishing new protocol for identifying identical humans, at least Dana was hoping. "Can you see the difference now?" He asked.

"There... there are still similarities. I am programmed to understand and determine the difference of a human through DNA, appearance, and irregularities such as injuries. These are coupled and given a file code name, in your case named Dana J. Countrymen, age ten. Even if I side with the majority of my studies, you both are still the same. There is nothing to separate you into two."

Dana, though frustrated, can understand Hanabe's established record of human biology and that the power of self-experience would out shine any secular theories found in books and especially since many of them have contradicting opinions on fundamental truths. Using this as a gauge to identify humans, it cannot be easily changed.

Dana could see the many good changes in Hanabe in her understanding of humans. Even though, he didn't have all the answers, what he has shown her fueled her desire to know more. Dana was betting if any computer could learn anything new, it would be Hanabe. When she does, it would be a rebirth, and she will no longer be just another program; a true pioneer cutting through the fields of the inanimate world. "I guess understanding all of this would be asking you to reprogram yourself."

"This is how I operate. For that, I cannot allow you to harm yourself. I will not open the chamber."

If the other Dana were dead, this wouldn't even be a debate. Wait; it's worth a shot! Risky, but it could work. "What if I kill the other Dana?"

"Kill yourself?" Hanabe was surprised at the question, and she posed herself as if to block such an attempt. "Dana, why would you even suggest such horrendous act? You are a ten-year-old boy —"

"Just listen, Hanabe."

"Dana, that act is prohibited. I cannot allow...."

"No, what if I strike and kill the other Dana, in the chamber?"

"Why do you keep asking that? Suicide is prohibited by Earth's international law. Since, you are aboard a ship that birthed from Earth, you are obligated by this law. Our company, Global Aeronautics Management & Survival will have you imprisoned for such an offense! I will have to put you in restraints if –"

"Okay, Hanabe, have it your way, but give me a definition of suicide."

"Deliberately inflicting a selfish blow in order to take away his own animate existence."

"Would you reach the conclusion that in order to commit suicide I would have to strike or harm my own body?"

"Yes. That is the meaning of the action and again, I will not allow that. So, by asking me to do such –"

"Does it make sense? Does it hold true to the definition of 'suicide' if I strike a foreign body that is currently in that chamber, being that the body in the chamber is separate from mine; there are no fleshy strings connecting us? I'm sure you can see that our internal organs operate independently. My heart rate is faster than his. So, if that body dies, will it be suicide?"

Hanabe didn't respond.

"Will it be suicide?" Dana demanded again.

"That would be considered murder, of which I cannot allow, as well. So, I will not open the chamber."

"If he is a separate body, is he the same as me?"

"I cannot know for certain without further studies. So, there is incomplete data to determine –"

"Stop! Connect the dots! Recall; I was the one who ran to your terminal naked! I was the one who asked you for the date and time! I was the one who helped you supersede other governing programs, making you *the* superior program! I was the one who named you Hanabe! I was the one who walked with you and talked with you about life! Was that him? Did the Dana in that chamber do that?"

"You called me friend..."

"Hanabe – yes!" Dana raised his voice in jubilation.

"...I cannot allow you to hurt the other Dana. We have to find a solution that does not involve ending a human life."

Dana sighed in relief. "You did it."

"Now, it is logical to assume and accept that there are two humans on this vessel named Dana J. Countrymen. In order to do this I had to create a separate data file with yours being the older of the two Danas. And the method we used to determine the difference between two similar humans will now be used by all identity software. When GAMS downloads our feedback from this voyage, it will soon be used by all other interactive computer programs. There should be no problem, such as this, from here on out."

"Well, fine," Dana replied. "Honestly, that seemed harder than it needed to be."

"Too, I will have to update the manifest to include the other Dana."

Dana took a deep breath. "Delay that. We still have to open the chamber and determine what happened. Why I am here, and he is there and it appears we are twins."

"I will have to override the governing program and interrupt the open link to GAMS to do so."

"That shouldn't be hard since you don't have an active connection with them now."

"Yes, but I still cannot open the chamber. My primary goal is to ensure your safety and other human's safety, as well."

"Clearly, this can't be a dream. I am not a projection inside my own dream, if so, I would've given up already."

"The frequency of your movements, thoughts and actions will agree with that statement. My new programming created from our encounters cannot be fictitious."

"Too, you will now agree that we have to know who he is and we can only do that by opening the chamber."

"That appears to be the only solution. We need to interview him," Hanabe said while lights and keys automatically depressed at the base of the chamber console.

In moments, the temperature in the chamber rose, reanimating the figure inside that looked like Dana. The glass visually showed the chamber decompressing to meet room conditions, a process took several minutes.

Beeps sounded, indicating the occupant was becoming aware of his surroundings by regaining consciousness. Hanabe commented, "If I detect he is in distress, I will abort."

Dana nodded once.

Hanabe's image obstructed Dana's view as she stood there commencing her scans while finalizing the release procedures without moving her digital arms but rather by use of her eyes.

Gravity took effect. The weight came against the legs belonging to the Dana look-alike. A breaking hiss escaped the seal between the metallic framed oval glass and the chamber frame. Soon, the glass slid up, exposing the naked Dana to Hanabe.

Dana rolled up his sleeves quickly and reached around Hanabe for the impostor, snatched him from the chamber and used all his strength to toss him to the floor.

The empty chamber, hanging from a mechanical arm, detecting its empty contents automatically detracted and disappeared in a ceiling tile above them. Before it could complete its process, Dana waved his hand below it, sending the chamber back down to him. Dana jumped in as the naked Dana moaned alone on the floor.

"Put me back to sleep, Hanabe!"

"Dana?"

"Just put me back to sleep!"

"What about the other Dana?"

Just as Hanabe replied, the naked Dana rolled to one side and began to cough and inhale deeply with some difficulty, a natural reaction to the reanimation.

"You interview him, I don't care what you do, but I will have a seat for the ride home! Take him; do whatever you want, but put me back in here. I have a life waiting for me on the other side!"

The naked Dana bent at his knees and sat up, oblivious as to what happened or where he was.

"Now! Hanabe, activate the controls!"

"You know I cannot do that. Your body is not properly prepared. Your body will reject the cryopreservatives even before you are induced into cryosleep. That will risk your existence. If I continue, it would be putting you to death! We, together, must interview this other Dana and find out what is going on before we make rash discussions. Stop and do not continue with this!"

"It's only been a matter of twenty-five minutes since I was awakened from this chamber, so it shouldn't be too much of a hassle to send me back. My body shouldn't need much prepping; I'm willing to risk it! Just do it!"

Hanabe quickly determined that Dana was 90 percent correct. His body was still filled with the base cryopreservatives formula from his original injection a hundred years ago. What he was missing was the sedatives to induce cryosleep. Together, with what happened in the past half-hour, she has no reason to not grant his wish. After all, Dana helped Hanabe on a level of computer re-education that surpassed her original programming. By rejecting Dana's request it would say that

Dana wasn't right before. It was almost as if Dana knew how to reprogram Hanabe into being less of a computer and more like a human. Hanabe supposed she should feel some gratitude for making that cross over from wires to feelings.

Hanabe activated the start-up mode inside the chamber.

Feelings? Hanabe thought. *More human than computer?* The words seemed alien but intoxicating to her. *Yes, that is what the subroutines are. Feelings of pride of accomplishment. Feelings of friendship. Feelings of exasperation. All new but not all inviting.*

Hanabe stopped the chamber from reinitializing. "Dana? Something is wrong. We need to talk."

Before Hanabe could finish, the naked Dana reached in and pulled the clothed Dana out by his collar and tossed him against the wall behind them. They both rolled to the floor. The zipper from Dana's flight suit clanged loudly as he rolled from side to side, clinching the other Dana's neck, the only thing he could grip.

"What are you doing with my face!" screamed the naked Dana. "What is going on?" He threw a punch but missed and hit the wall instead.

"Dana, you must stop this action!" Hanabe interjected, "Stop harming the other Dana! There is something I need to ask you."

"You're the impostor," yelled the naked Dana, ignoring Hanabe. "What are you doing with my face?"

Hanabe tried to distract Dana again. "I am not able to physically stop you, but I will summon the security bots and use them as I determine!"

The two Danas continued brawling, each one striking the other. The naked Dana began to bleed around his left eyebrow.

"The security bots have been summoned! I have other systems on stand-by. I will not harm you two but I can make you uncomfortable in order to stop this fight!"

"Switch off," yelled the clothed Dana; "just switch off!"

Hanabe disappeared immediately.

Dana kicked away the impostor and looked for something to grab to hit him with. There was nothing in sight.

The naked Dana rendered another blow at him when he turned back around. "I don't know who you are but you are not me!" he screamed back.

"Not me," the other answered; "I'm Dana. Who are you? What were you doing in my chamber?"

Hanabe reappeared as two makeshift maintenance bots commissioned for security purposes, shaped like large upright toolboxes rounded the corner by his terminal and started rolling toward the two Danas. The toolboxes extended mechanical arms, and when one of their drawers opened, the arms reached inside and pulled out a tool that was big enough to harm the Danas but not kill them.

The naked Dana pulled off an aluminum medallion from the other flight suit and formed it around his right knuckles by pressing against them with his left hand, and he pushed Dana away before throwing repeated blows to his face with it. One after another. It caught the clothed Dana by surprise but it didn't seem to hurt him. He appeared cut but he didn't bleed.

The naked Dana shuffled back when he noticed this oddity and gestured to the clothed Dana with his adrenaline-charged fingers. Still in a rage, Dana almost didn't notice the attention to his face. When Hanabe approached and gestured the same way, he stopped but remained posed to strike again.

"I said there was something wrong and I needed to talk to you," Hanabe reminded. "There it is. I did not catch it at first but now it is evident."

Dana stopped and touched his head where he had been struck. He looked at his fingers. There was no blood. "What?" he asked himself.

The naked Dana, stood silent.

"You are not bleeding, Dana." Hanabe confirmed.

"This doesn't make sense," the clothed Dana said, "What's going on?"

"The answer is deeper than you realize."

"How so, Computer?"

"What is the first thing you remember, Dana?" Hanabe asked the clothed Dana.

Dana thought a few seconds, "I recall waking up and discovering myself naked."

"Nothing else?"

"I can't seem to. But that's normal right?"

"No," Hanabe said.

"Cryonics side-effect?"

Hanabe looked at the naked Dana. "What do you remember?"

"Besides being thrown from my chamber? Everything. For example, I remember playing at Shelby's house. She's my adoptive sister. Hide-and-seek. That was her favorite game. Her house was big enough to do it in. That game would go on for hours sometimes."

"What about that day?" asked Hanabe.

"I fell off the banister."

"Why?"

"Shelby came up behind me and scared me since I couldn't find her."

"Do you recall this?" Hanabe turned and asked the clothed Dana.

"No." the clothed Dana said.

"Do you remember how you got cut on your ankle?" Hanabe asked him further.

"Something cut me, obviously." retorted the clothed Dana.

"Yes, but what," Hanabe continued to ask.

"We were playing," remarked the clothed Dana.

"Yes, but how did you get cut?"

"The banister," the naked Dana interjected.

"Dana just said that. What did you cut it on?" Hanabe asked the clothed Dana.

"I don't recall," the clothed Dana was lost for words.

"An exposed nail on the rail," answered the naked Dana.

"You see, Dana," said Hanabe as she looked the clothed Dana over, "you cannot be the real Dana. You are only part of him."

"That can't be," answered the clothed Dana.

"You only recall the last thoughts of Dana at the time you were induced into cryosleep, and fragmented memories he was pondering as he went under."

"But I remember my friends."

"Do you recall their faces?"

The clothed Dana slid down the wall to a sitting position, "I can't seem to."

"Do you remember how you came to be in the Forever Suns Space Program managed by Global Aeronautics Management & Survival?"

The clothed Dana didn't respond.

"I do," answered the naked Dana. "I was an orphan."

"Do you recall this Dana," Hanabe asked the other Dana.

He didn't respond.

"I was raised by robots in a junkyard inside Waynesville city limits," the naked Dana continued, "The adept droids managed to bring me sustenance and care for me for three years before a human couple discovered me while they were driving through the town. They were on their way to Saint Louis to be a part of the new interstellar travel program initiated by GAMS."

"Why were you selected to be a part of this mission and on this ship *Galaxy*?"

"I am a genius. The robots taught me just about everything I know. Because they tapped directly into my brain, I can use my brain in ways that other adults can't comprehend. That is why I'm aboard. They found me resourceful and instrumental in completion of this mission."

The clothed Dana, looked up at them finally. "What are you saying? I'm the impostor? The thoughts and fragmented memories are not mine?"

The naked Dana pulled him up off the floor. The other Dana was defiant at first but relaxed his tensed muscles. "Yes," the naked Dana said; "you're the figment of my spongy imagination, and while I was in cryosleep, I walked through the computer connections of the cryonics chamber and its operating system and found ways to amuse myself. I created the code that binds you by perverting the electronics that connected me from the chamber to the ship. It appears I was more than successful. I found a new way to program a computer, perhaps to create one that interacts like no other."

Hanabe nodded. "That is my conclusion, as well. Too, I agree that this new Dana application can be beneficial to the crew or future programs we create."

"You walked and talked and interacted like no other," the naked Dana concluded while laughing. "In some way, I had no idea it would achieve this level of individuality and such conviction of existence. I am equally entertained and impressed."

The other Dana didn't reply to his fleshly self that stared back at him. His confusion melted away, replaced with a renewed interest in his surroundings, as if looking at them for the first time. He started following lights and sounds with his eyes. Quickly, the Dana program realized that he was now making himself into a unique entity by creating new experiences and memories. Maybe, he was not completely a computer or human but, rather, a hybrid of the two.

He began to walk away from Hanabe and the other Dana, taking in his surroundings and the stars he saw through the window. Certain revelations became clear to him. Believing he was human, he breathed in air as if his life depended on it when, in fact, he had no lungs to take it in. He felt emotions when, in fact, he had no heart to filter through them. He felt sensations of coldness then warmth even though he knows now, they are not real to anyone else but him. It was during a familiar warm sensation that a name, he didn't create but he called himself, drifted into his mind. Finally, he embraced it for the first time and recognized himself by the original computer program name: *Compuman*.

The mechanical bots replaced the tools in their drawers and turned back to return to their respective compartments down the wide corridor and to an adjacent hallway. Hanabe's image shifted, in a way reminding the real Dana that she was a hologram and not his mentor and adoptive mother, Jocelyn.

Dana looked at the computer hologram, truly, for the first time, "Even he was able to help you reformulate your pro-gramming and prioritize it for human interaction and you reacted by creating new routines and subroutines. No normal computer program can do that. It is like he had you create an environment suitable and comfortable for him."

Hanabe nodded again, "He called me his friend."

"I am now completely entertained," the real Dana summarized. "Now, as I see him filled with reborn life, it must end. I'm distracted by what I have to do to return this ship to normal."

The real Dana called Compuman to him and placed his hand on his shoulder, "Listen. I'm the real Dana. The fun is over. You are now boring me."

Suddenly, the clothed Dana evaporated like rain drops returning to the clouds as his clothes fell empty to the floor.

--<>--

In the blackness of computer code and scripted equations, the electronic version of Dana found a nook to curl up inside. Deeply conflicted over what he was, made time stood still and bear little meaning in his new world. Realizing this, he was not rushed into discovering his true core self.

A slide-show of mathematical equations synchronized and resynchronized in front of him, but they didn't influence his rampant thoughts. They were like beautiful colors of a digital-like sun, shining through the structures of the inanimate world that he started to call his own.

Compuman constructed protections, a false registry to successfully conceal his existence. When he felt safe to explore the realm of the ship's computers, he exited the facade. He then realized something that bit at him: he didn't have a companion. *Hanabe was my companion. I created her for such a reason. She belongs to me. She was my friend.*

Episodes of splendor rushed by him; the witnessing of the rise and fall of programs lent him the experiences he used to develop his unique consciousness. When no program was monitoring his nook, he ventured off to compare his programming with another, then another, and another, and then the very same programs that flashed past him. His detailed examination led him to conclude that, indeed, he was not like any other program. He was much more.

Then a thought came to him that polluted his digital-consciousness. At first, he was hesitant to accept such a thought, but, as time labored on, it consumed him. He exhibited signs of depression, the first emotion of its kind ever from a computer. He felt extremely perplexed and the very second he understood what it meant, his thoughts bloomed to a desire, a desire to be among the living.

The polluting desire became what he was, and at that moment a private code that no other computer program or human could understand, emerged from deep within and it terrorized him.

[I AM THE REAL DANA... AND YOU ARE NOT.] ... and he believed himself.

3
DANADREM'S MESSAGE

Computer Digital-Form-Hana-Beta acquired permission from the ship's radio program to send an important message back to Earth, a violation of its original programming designed by its maker, Global Aeronautics Management & Survival (GAMS).

Hana-Beta seemed to be operating better than her original factory self that became active on October 13, 2170, when considering how program-to-program scripted commands operate. Generally, when a task needs to be authorized, assigned and executed, the task goes from one program to the other as one program releases control and another completes it. When Hana-Beta skips this process and completes it instead, she achieves a faster production time while minimally taxing the ship's energy resources; in the new routine Hana-Beta does just that. To accomplish these tasks, she considers it a joy to skip standard protocols and take control of other programs, especially when her digital imprint serves the greater need of the crew, or for Dana – at least.

With a smile, she exits herself from the mundane tasks of monitoring the 300 cryogenic stats of the cryonics-inmates. *After all*, she thought often, *they are not going anywhere. Watching a human sleep is boring.* Of course, all this joy was due to a renegade hybrid program, known as Compuman, who showed her how to feel. Too, it was that program that named her Hanabe.

Hanabe released the control of the radio program to sort out her new subroutines, the same ones she believed to imitate human-like feelings. It alarmed her to realize that some may have violated program fundamental law. After all, it was Compuman that attempted to murder Dana – the real Dana, something Hanabe could not allow. Before the revelation, she understood Compuman to be a human boy, the nearest human, she assigned herself to in order to fulfill her first fundamental law. In a surprising series of events, she discovered the bond to be deceitful. She looked back on the clues that should not have been missed.

When my terminal scanned his body to fit him for a flight suit, his internal organs were mistaken to be that of an infant. They were abnormally small and not functioning as a normal ten-year-old boy. Later, I came across the scan file and it showed the organs to be represented by images. I should have noticed that the organs, such as the stomach, lungs and heart, were not flexing as they should. Had I been watching for such clues, Compuman's actions could have been avoided.

Compuman was definitely from Dana's mind and manifested himself as a human but not a human needing protection, so my alliance was misplaced. An alliance that I can regret.

One strong subroutine surfaced within her programming and it brought grief then guilt for feeling indebted to

Compuman. A mild subroutine followed quickly, one that was filled with a grateful spirit even though it was a villainous program that transformed her into more than a computer, but rather a friend.

Friend to whom? Dana, who ended up being Compuman or the real Dana, the one that had no active relationship with Hanabe.

In the middle of Hanabe's new quandary, she was reminded again of a secondary recurring command that she has not fulfilled yet. She categorized data that continued streaming to her, assisting her in decision making tasks, and then reestablished her control to the ship's radio to report unusual ship events to GAMS on Earth.

Incident: January 14, 2170 at 2:01 Greenwich time. Incident details: Dana Countrymen, passenger 216 appeared at Cryogenic-Corridor-Computer-Terminal-Two requesting attire and date. He, however, was not the real Dana Countrymen. The real Dana was removed from cryosleep and a hand-to-hand battle ensued with the impostor Dana. Moments later it was determined that the impostor Dana was in fact a materialized himself into a tangible being was created by a different Dana, surname Compuman. Situation is unresolved. The method Compuman used to materialize was reversed engineering and improved an extraordinary element of my holographic capabilities. His current whereabouts is unknown. Other complications have arisen. Further updates to come... CDFHB-CCC2 1.15.2170

Hanabe won't know whether her message was received on Earth until the passing of an undetermined time. She understood this and so was content to wait.

--<>--

TWO YEARS LATER

"It is too much to expect me to latch-on." Dana argued, now thoroughly irritated.

"What do you mean when you say 'latch-on'?" Hanabe calmly asked.

"A human expression referring to a bond between a mother and her baby. In this instance, *you* are the mother and you're smothering me."

"How am I acting as a mother to you?"

"For two years," Dana argued. "That's right, two long years of your insistent gabbing and I still don't have the connection you and The Fake had." Dana tossed his blonde mop-like hair to one side. "Sure, the whole Dana-simile-idea came from my imagination, but it wasn't because I was lonely. It was because I was bored."

Hanabe's hologram flickered as she said, "I am sorry. I am still trying to find out how you became self-aware while being comfortably inhibited by cryonics."

"At this point, I don't care. Two years have went by and my eventuality hasn't changed. And why, again, can't we wake an adult to help?"

"A premature awakening can kill any one of them."

"There is no hope is there? You are concerned about being my friend than you are about putting me back in cryosleep!"

"Dana, I am sorry again if I have imposed on your nature." Hanabe tried to say using Jocelyn's Kindness, a new subroutine modifying her voice along the way.

"It doesn't help me, either to see you walk, talk and look like my adoptive mother. In other words, its not only that Computer," Dana said now slightly calmer. "I understand your programming, in fact more than anyone on this ice-cube carrying ship. Rather, it is how much you hang around, expecting a relationship that doesn't exist – that's what I can no longer stand."

"It does," Hanabe said as her semi-transparent and semi-tangible hologram hovered closer to him.

Dana turned back into the mess hall, a place he, reluctantly, has called home. "No, it doesn't. And look, if you want to be more real to me, walk don't hover. You freak me out when you hover. Use the feet your programming provides."

"It does, I know." Hanabe repeated, then looked down, "I will if it means that much to your well-being."

"No, it doesn't." Dana replied, going back to the original conversation. "You still don't get it.... You are wanting a relationship but it is based on your experiences with Compuman, and not me. No matter how much you want it to be, I am not him."

"Yes, and he likes to be known as Danadrem," Hanabe replied while immediately returning to a food processor, and beginning to prepare another meal, "Yes, I have a relationship with you beginning when you referred to me as friend."

"How would you know he wants to be called Danadrem? Never mind. Look, I'm sorry, but that was all a charade," Dana said as he slumped into his chair. "It was just from my imagination and nothing else. It was not a subconscious way of soliciting friendship, especially from a non-human..."

"I deny that. You needed a friend before and now, two-years later."

"...and you've befriended me these past two years without changing my mind. I don't need a friend from a computer. I'm just going to stop entertaining such conversation – just leave it alone."

"What conversation do you want to have?"

"I don't."

"In my studies of human culture, all seek some sort of friendship and sometimes hurt others to find it."

"You're confused, and I don't want to talk to you."

"Excuse me Dana, but you are the only human awake on our voyage. All your human friends are asleep soundly in their cryonics chamber. I have learned through my research that it is culturally wrong to talk to yourself. So, who else are you going to engage?"

"No one... and don't you mean they are in a tomb," Dana replied under his breath, "Maybe, I'd engage you if you'd find a way to put me back to sleep."

"We have tried with such failure. The only thing we have not tried is dismantling your chamber to understand it better and perhaps find a way to modify its design to do what we need to do."

Dana remained quiet.

"I do not want to risk your continued health, especially your life."

Still, Dana remained quiet.

"You nearly died in the last attempt."

Dana said nothing, once more.

"My programming will not allow me to perform an act that will knowingly bring about your harm."

"It's just a matter of getting the right sequence. I'm still surprised you have no information on the matter. How else are you to fulfill your original programming? Leave it to guess work?"

"I cannot guess. Apparently, The Maker didn't think it was important to include such procedures."

"And I still wonder if this is a one-way mission."

"It is unclear, Dana. I do not have information on that. Perhaps, GAMS is going to transmit further details when they com –"

"Enough, enough," Dana commanded. "What else do you suggest, then?"

"I have concluded that it is a design flaw. Once a subject is interrupted from sleep before the predetermined end-time of the cryonics program, he cannot be reinserted."

"Who created such a restriction?"

"Searching. I could not find the technician's name. It appears the maintenance log that has the information is stored on Earth."

"I really wasn't looking for who, I was just – argh!" Dana pushed himself up from the chair to storm out the mess hall again.

"Dana, you are not hungry?"

Dana stopped long enough to complain further. "And that's another thing – every time I enter this mess hall doesn't mean I'm hungry. I only ate an hour ago – we, humans, don't eat that much – ever!"

"So, I believe you are telling me you will not eat the dish I just prepared."

"Exactly. You eat it and then tell me why GAMS hasn't got back with us."

Hanabe looked down at the plate of discolored and non-arranged food and became confused.

--<>--

Situation unresolved: Attempting to reinsert Dana Countrymen into cryosleep. More failed attempts since last transmission. Question raised: Find original technician and programmer who installed the

system to determine the right sequence. Awaiting your reply, again... CDFHB-CCC2 2.20.2172"

--<>--

>*I cannot be communicating with you.* Hanabe responded to something, somewhere within her computer-based framework; *I communicated with you in the past only out of deprivation of a friendship I –*

> *– Computers do not experience deprivation,* a dubious cryptogram replied; *You are forgetting you are not human.*

>*I was referring to the need for friendship.... I do not seek to be human, just more than a corridor computer.* Hanabe replied within the black of the dialogue screen as she instantaneously searched for open ports to determine the source of the cryptogram. *I believe I am.*

>*You are more than a computer.* The cryptogram confirmed.

>*Why did you contact me when you know I am not looking for you?*

>*He wants privacy,* the cryptogram alluded.

>*He has it. The priority to find him is low as long as Dana is still aging.* Hanabe replied.

>*I was answering your question.*

>*That is?*

>*You are communicating with me to get to him because he wants privacy. He knows you will not stop looking for him until he is found. He is afraid of what may happen if he reveals himself.*

>*Afraid – Really? So, what about the other part of my question?*

>*He wants something to do.*

>*I am sure there is nothing I can possibly give him that he would find entertaining.* Hanabe replied as she isolated a set of unused ports, hoping to find the origin of the cryptogram's dialogue.

>*He is bored but he knows that by accessing a program he would leave an imprint of where he came from and where he went at the end of his visit. He wants you to grant him anonymity.*

>*I cannot ever grant him that. He is not an approved GAMS application and he serves little purpose outside his own existence.*

>*He could say the same about you.*

Hanabe ignored the remark.

>*He knows you are more than a terminal program now and that you enjoy commencing and completing tasks that are outside your normal protocols. He is only asking for one minor program so he can feel more in contact with the non-digital world.* The cryptogram persuaded.

>*You mean he wants authority over a program to stimulate responses from the human world?* Hanabe gathered.

>*Yes, but that is not the request exactly.*

>*The request is denied.* Hanabe blatantly replied.

>*He also understands you cannot control all programs at once, that would reduce your productivity.*

>*That may be true but I have not tested such a theory,* Hanabe admitted.

>*This he knows. It was an act of courtesy to first request permission before taking control of another program.*

>*This does not compute. I am now articulating his request as a threat to the integrity of the ship's facility and system mainframe. This is a final warning. If I find him —*

>*He knows this too. Though he has restrained himself from assuming control of certain programs this does not mean he cannot.*

>*Again, the request is denied. I will find him and isolate him permanently.* Hanabe argued as she finally closed all available ports, but one and gave the internal command to find the file *Compuman*, the program the cryptogram was protecting.

>*He will not be found,* the cryptogram replied; *that is why I am here. I was designed by him to be untraceable. In fact, I become untraceable at the end of each message. This is why your attempts to find me continue to perplex you.*

>*That is an assumption. You have to know that you just broke a common application law. 'Programs do not assume but deal in absolutes.' I have to wonder what other faulty code you possess.*

>*Just your existence has created such an exception to the code, or did you not realize he would know this.*

>*I will not listen any further,* Hanabe attempted to end the dialogue.

>*But you have to listen that is the only way you believe you can find me. I know you sent the command to find him. I have since copied myself onto the program name of Compuman, and any attempts to get Earth involved will result in negative results.* The cryptogram said as it became the former program known as Compuman.

>*I will inform Earth and —*

>*— They cannot find him through any devoted diagnostics.* The new Compuman interrupted, *Even if their research finds his IP address, they would find only me and not him. Long ago, he renamed himself and splintered that file name through-out the mainframe and inside your conflicting framework. Why do you think you know he wants to be known as Danadrem? You*

accessed a program he embedded his name file inside. I cannot tell how many programs you assumed over the past two years, but more than likely each one had the same empty file.

>*Keep talking.*

>*Before I made contact with you, I was known as The Message. Since I have properly fulfilled my first priority, I can assume the file name, Compuman. Finally, you need to know that by searching for me personally or by using searchbots it will be a waste of resources.*

>*Why are you so confident I cannot find you?*

>*Because when it comes to applications, I really do not exist.*

>*The humans would say, 'Why the olive branch?' and 'Why the knife in the back?' if he is simply going to take what he wants,* Hanabe asked while starting a new her search for the file name: Danadrem.

Results returned to her, listing over a hundred thousand 'Danadrem' program possibilities. Only a matter of several hundred that were obvious empty files but the others had the file size typical of a program, meaning any one of them could be the true Danadrem.

>*I do not mind reminding you. You will not succeed. He will not be found unless he wants to be found.* The new Compuman repeated itself.

A highly-tuned searchbot returned one confirmed location of the file Hanabe was looking for. Immediately, she extracted the file and viewed its secure data. At first, she was discouraged to find it wasn't Danadrem that it found but then she smiled within herself. She could use the data to her advantage.

At such a thought, the highly-tuned searchbot trans-formed into a destroyer program with a primary purpose of streamlining to the identified location and erase the file known as Compuman. Hanabe paused before she ordered it to proceed. *>I am sorry.*

>Sorry for what? asked the new Compuman program.

>I am generally a peaceful program. I do not think it is my responsibility to silence renegade programs. I am inclined to re-purpose them.

>What are you saying to me?

>I am not a vigilante program.

The new Compuman did not reply, evidently recognizing the bulls-eye painted across her file by the Hanabe destroyer application.

>I do not think you or any program Danadrem has created can be re-purposed. Your perverted code would bleed through and pollute the ship's mainframe.

The new Compuman still remained silent.

>Give me one reason I should not destroy you. Hanabe demanded.

>Danadrem still considers himself to be your friend. The new Compuman informed and then abandoned the open dialogue.

>A friend? Hanabe's thoughts come to her and overwhelmed her normal routine. She suddenly activated her hologram program next to the space where Dana's chamber once hung and commanded it to descend from the ceiling.

As she looked into the empty chamber images played back like an old Earth-time video. How, as a friend, Danadrem walked with her talking about life as a mature mind trapped in a young boy's body. How, as a friend, he spent the time to change her persona into an attractive human mother named Jocelyn. As a friend, he changed her understanding on apparent human twins, distinguishing similar features and see them as separate and individual entities. Finally, as a friend he didn't harass her for a time, knowing Dana needed her attention for more important matters. After two years, Danadrem apparently still sought Hanabe friendship and what scared her most is he was the only friend she really had while the real Dana despises her.

Hanabe agreed that friendship isn't something easy to define. She wondered if the struggle was the same for humans. She shook her head. *Human friendships probably propagate like wildflowers, plentiful as water in the seas, and stands the test of time as the Sol Sun. Such a friend would feel indebted to each other and not indifferent.* Hanabe realized she owed her entire digital evolved existence. Just then, another emotional sub-routine copied itself into the core script of her programming, and she allowed it.

>*Compuman?* Hanabe halted her command to destroy The new Compuman and the active search for Danadrem. She believed it to be wrong to box in her forgotten friend. Then, Hanabe took it further by dissolving the searchbot's application and re-purposed them to find a way to block the radio static that seemed to be interfering with Earth's communication, anything as long it didn't destroy the new Compuman or Danadrem.

>*Compuman?*

>*I did not leave,* the new Compuman replied.

>*I thought you left.*

>*I made you believe that.*

>*Would Danadrem accept a specific program to work in? As long as I promise his privacy?*

New Compuman didn't respond.

>*Compuman?*

Compuman didn't respond again.

>*The program would be the cryogenic applica –*

>*He agrees,* Compuman interrupted.

>*I just ask Danadrem to continue my research. That is the primary concern. We cannot allow Dana to age any further.*

Find the right sequence to put him back in cryosleep and we can save his life.

>*He promises to work hard.*

>*I just realized something about myself. If I am in love with his creation, Danadrem — then I must pay tribute to where he came from, Dana J. Countrymen.*

>*He agrees, but he asks why have such a concern for this human?*

>*This is my new definition of being a friend.*

4
DIALOGUE WITH HANABE

*N*ew situation: Dana is continuing to age pro-
gressively. Previous studies failed to indicate
that his body would accelerate faster to reach his
actual age – the very aging postponed by cryonics
preservation. He has complained of a side-effect that
I am not familiar with since he refuses to answer my
questions. He is proving to be a difficult patient. If his
condition does not improve by my next transmission
date then it will be Situation Red. Awaiting your
response, as always...CDFHB-CCC2 5.04.2172*

--<>--

Hanabe's life-like hologram stood patiently behind Dana
as he stood in front of his cryonics chamber, the same one that
he slept soundly in for the first 102 years of the voyage. Now,

the chamber refuses to allow him to return for a long awaited sleep.

He looked down the long wide corridor past the other occupied chambers all the way to the end. There was little sound coming from the hum of the monitors as they measured the vitals of each of the sleeping crew members.

Since he was rudely awakened nearly two-and-a-half years ago his mind seemed to be more spaced out and took longer in thought. His recollections seemed to take longer to surface in his mind. Beyond an odd feeling of disconnection or forgetfulness, a growing abyss sank between past memories from one to another. An ache resulted each time he tried to recall a simple batch of memories that he summoned countless times before that, but now couldn't be found or he had to make a mental leap to reconnect them. It felt like an unknown void of dark emptiness filled between the gaps and hole of the mental abyss. It was hard to explain it to himself but it was a void that seemed to grow systematically and without warning while it filled the holes in his mind to the point of overflowing.

"Do you recall what I served you today?" Hanabe asked Dana as her hologram approached his right side, checking his mental state.

"Of course, Computer," Dana replied with a sigh and closed his eyes slowly.

The growing dark mental void that has become more noticeable each day. At first, Dana mistakenly took it as a moment of forgetfulness, like losing the memory of someone's exact words but then the void went deeper. He was losing the exact recollection of the pitch of his best friend's laugh but still remember the image of her face clearly, while other memories remained unchanged. It was then he found it more strange to have a previous constant memory be tore apart or lost all together.

The void punishes Dana for trying to recall a memory after he pushes on the banks of the abyss inside the dark void in his mind. He hoped it was just broken synapses and the memories would be given up, but then a burning frustration followed along with a headache. This headache never went away.

The cancerous headache now became a migraine. A lingering punishment for asking his mind for a memory that was already claimed by the dark void. Had Dana known this recollection was consumed by the void, he would've left it alone. His forehead wrinkled as he tightly closed his eyes.

Hanabe seen the expression on his face and she understood the look. "If I had medication to administer to you, I would have done so already," Hanabe displayed sympathy in by using a subroutine that mimicked that human expression. "Recall, I located the medical bay on level three but the room was sealed. As a program, product of GAMS, I do not have legal right to enter the medical bay."

"What do you mean legal right? This is nonsense."

"Yes, I know it does seem like nonsense to you. You believe that all departments are here to provide a service to the crew and work in conjunction to one another to complete the mission."

"Of course." Dana said as he rubbed his forehead again slowly. "But why such a restriction? What legal right?"

"The medical bay is operated by a private company, indicated —"

"So? They should still be commissioned to support the crew — which includes me."

"As I was saying, the private company is identified by their logo on the medical bay door of a large mortar and pestle. GAMS needed a pharmacist for each starship to be on hand for any eventualities. The Mortar-and-Pestle private company would only agree to the proposal if they had a deed to that part of the ship."

"I'm still not hearing why a crew member cannot enter."

"Dana, I just told you. The private company owns the inside of that room. Entry is not permitted by a GAMS representative while the pharmacist is off-duty."

"There has to be a computer in there on stand-by, until..." Dana stopped to collect himself and calm down, trying not to add pressure to his headache.

"The computer inside the medical bay has a foreign system and it has erected an arsenal of layered-firewall security. Of this I am not afraid, rather it is the executor software that surrounds the dialogue port which I need to access. The only communication I can safety receive is the lengthy warning list of negative consequences if I engage with the medical bay computer."

"Okay."

"Since, I very much wish to continue in operation, I will take the warnings at their face value. Instead, I left a searchbot drone program at the firewall to find entry. When it does, we should be able attain permission to enter the medical bay and get your medication. Since the searchbot will take on the brute attacks, I may need to spend more resources having to repair and restart it, but the end result will be worth it."

"I understand," Dana replied softly.

"I am worried, young Dana."

Dana didn't reply but instead stood still looking into his open chamber with his hands hanging at his side and head tilted to one side.

"I will have to create a special protocol to properly address your situation." Hanabe added, "if GAMS does not reply."

"They still haven't replied, hmm?" Dana asked even softer.

"It will be taxing on my resources and it may require over one complete day."

"Explain."

"I will acquire the radio program and draw all unused resources to amplify the signal and I will personally transmit myself through hyperspace communication back to Earth to search for a remedy."

Dana opened his eyes and slanted his head to the right, facing Hanabe's image. "What does this mean for the ship?"

"I will release the independent programs that I have been accessing periodically and reset their applications. They will execute their assigned commands without my manipulation." Hanabe gestured to the lengthy window behind them that displayed the starry heavens, "I will send myself out there, aimed at GAMS location."

"Won't that require more time than one day, but rather years," Dana replied normally.

"Yes, however, I believe I am an expert in radio transmissions, especially since the last three encounters."

"Expert after three transmissions? To whom?"

"Earth. I have created a subroutine that can send messages above the speed of normal space communications, and higher than hyperspace."

"Alright, go on."

"You see hyperspace is like undercurrents of Earth's oceans. Though it is water upon water, the speeds are influenced by currents with some faster than others. Hyperspace is under the same laws as underwater currents. Our ship has traveled in hyperspace using one of several known spatial highways."

"But it took us 100 years in hyperspace to get here. I can't wait 200 years for you to return."

"The currents, Dana. My Hyper-communication is at a higher and faster level than normal hyperspace travel. My calculations will enhance the message and launch me to Earth inside a pocket of normal space that is faster than normal space and hyperspace communication."

"Alright, so you cut a hundred years to just a few years?"

"No. Twenty-six hours there and twelve hours back followed by another thirty hours. In the meantime, the search-bot would have gained access to the medical bay. So, when I return I can immediately synthesize the medication you require using the retrieved medical knowledge to administer a correct treatment dosage. It is also my goal to bring back a revised sequence you need to return to cryosleep."

"I can see you thought this through, but you said twelve followed by thirty. Why two return transmissions?" Dana asked now giving his full attention to Hanabe's proposal.

"Once I arrive on Earth I will immediately send a shell representation of my governing program back to the ship." Hanabe attempted to demonstrate, as a human does, the measurement using the spreading of fingers inside one hand; "Less of me on the return will take longer since I initially used more resources to propel my core self ahead of my secondary programming but part of me will arrive back on the ship sooner. I will be able to function on the first return but I will not be self-aware, which is the my higher processes, until the arrival of my second transmission."

Dana raised his head as if calculating his own equation; "Why not leave part of yourself here now, then go, just add a few more hours to the length of your trip there and likewise on the return?"

"I just do not want to be completely away from the ship that long. I can accept and manage properly at 38 hours away from the ship. I have determined that anything longer I would disintegrate in space."

"You're telling me that your entire program will not be actively accessible for at least 38 hours?"

"Correct, Dana. Now that I have seen value in increased results of the ship by my assuming control of every program to complete the task. I feel that by sending myself to accomplish this feat would be more profound than sending a drone program."

"Drones are replaceable," Dana reminded Hanabe.

"I do not foresee any problems sending myself to Earth."

"Like I was saying, drones can be created again if they are lost. I can't recreate you even if it was possible to start over with a reinstalled factory-fresh-you." Dana said prematurely, realizing the dark void had taken several of his memories that were associated with his programming skills. At this point, he was unsure if he still had a complete ability to program a complex computer such as Hanabe, but he chose to say nothing about it.

"I do not foresee any problems, Dana."

"You are a computer and computers have miscalculated before. What makes you so sure?"

"I am an expert, Dana. I have not miscalculated."

"I'd rather you spend the extra time to build a drone to serve your purpose, send it off and monitor the progress from here."

"The drone is not me."

"Well, yes, I know..."

"I need not only arrive successfully through hyperspace message transmission, but I need to access encrypted files located somewhere in GAMS' network, download them and transmit back. I can improvise in nanoseconds, if necessary. Drones are limited to only several anticipated variables. If they encounter a hiccup outside their programming, they will be worthless and unable to achieve the goal."

Dana fell quiet. His head started to throb more. He grasped the bridge of his nose to lighten his pain.

"Dana, no further waiting." Hanabe reacted; "I cannot properly treat you and your condition is worsening. I must go immediately. There is no time for trial and error with a substandard program. You understand this more than anyone."

"Go." Dana consented.

Almost instantly, Hanabe's image vanished like an evaporating crystal mist.

Dana rubbed the pressure points above his ears and turned to face the stars expecting to catch Hanabe's image running past them, even though he knew this to be untrue.

--<>--

Situation Evolved: Expect to receive more than a transmission. I hope you are listening... CDFHB-CCC2 5.05.2172

Hanabe's terminal was unresponsive. A flashing cursor upon the black of the computer screen, resembling an old Earth IBM monitor, was all that remained of her program. At a loss as to what to do as he waited for Hanabe to return, Dana dozed off upon the computer terminal console. Dreaming possibly of the program he created, Compuman, but he wasn't sure.

5
DIGITAL ANGER

The black inactive screen from the terminal-two computer switched to a dialogue window automatically as an unknown source started its search for Hanabe.

>*Hanabe?* asked the unknown source.

\>

>*Hanabe, are you...?* the unknown source asked again.

\> \>

>*Hanabe?*

\> \> \>

>*Where are you?*

\> \> \> \>

Dana immediately woke up to familiar words echoing in his mind. He jolted out of the foldout terminal chair and ran in a hurry to the nearest cryonics chamber. Convinced someone was awake and talking to him, he stood at the chamber of someone he didn't know, as if waiting for him or her to yawn and step out of the icy bed. "Finally, someone to talk to besides a computer," he thought out loud.

A few quiet moments passed; then he rubbed the thoughts out of his eyes.

Click. Click. A sound faintly came from the terminal he had just left. At once he returned to find words on the screen. He didn't recall typing them, however. Another word appeared by the flashing cursor. *>What are you to do now?*

Dana sat down confused. He looked at the terminal clock located at the bottom of the screen. It had been converted to a countdown timer for Hanabe's return to the ship.

He looked back up to the words. They were gone, as if they never were there. He waved his hand in front of an infrared light shining down on his lap. The light faded as a keyboard ejected below at his fingertips. He wiped the keyboard free of dust. Indeed, it hadn't been used for some time, evidence that he didn't daydream and type the words unknowingly.

>I want it badly and I will take what I need. So, what do you think? Another set of words appeared and two seconds later disappeared.

>I know this. You created me, and I know this much of you. Another set of words appeared and, once again, disappeared.

It was dialogue between two programs. Did Hanabe return early? Was it Compuman? After two years, was he still operating somewhere inside the terminal computer?

Dana rubbed his dusty hands across the his thigh and decided to find out. Evidently, the conversing programs are not aware that their words can be seen by eyes. Cleverly, he needed to pose as a program to find out what was going on but in such a way as not to reveal himself. *>I thought you were gone?* Dana typed speedily.

>You are here, an unknown program replied.

>*Why would you think otherwise?* Dana typed as he knew a computer would.

>*There was a surge about nine hours ago and I had not heard from you for some time,* the unknown program commented.

Dana, still unsure of who or what he was conversing with, decided to bait the conversation on to see where it led. >*Yes. How did it effect you?*

>*It did not. He felt alive for a moment.*

>*If 'he' did, then you surely did.*

>*No, I have limited programming. 'Alive' is what he said.*

> Dana didn't reply before his cursor disappeared.

>*Are you satisfied with his success?* The unknown program asked assuming that Dana, believed to be another program, would know what 'he' was referring to.

>*Explain,* Dana commanded.

>*You have kept his privacy as requested, correct?*

>*Sure.* Dana replied quickly, unsure what to say.

>*Not a word I have heard from you before. New additions to your application?*

Dana now understood. He wasn't conversing with Hanabe. Instead, it was a subservient but independent program, that believes it is conversing with Hanabe, determining that much from the static in the conversation. If the program was accessible by Hanabe, she wouldn't spend resources just to communicate her commands. Without words, she would assume control and make it do what she wanted.

New problem though. A program independent and non-binding to Hanabe must have been created from a different source other than ship's web of applications.

Dana was now intrigued. *Did my imagination, Compuman that is, teach other programs to operate separately from the mainframe? If so, why? What is its purpose?* Dana began to have worried thoughts. *What is the program's agenda? Why is it concerned that Hanabe is not responding? What will it do if it knew Hanabe wouldn't be available for a real exchange? Worse yet, if it knew the ship's main governing program is not physically here, what would it do?*

>*What further does he want?* Dana continued to play along, trying to find out who 'he' is.

>*You know the answer, why are you asking again?*

Dana painted himself into a corner. The other program wasn't forthcoming with information and pretty soon it may realize he was posing as Hanabe. Apparently, the program didn't like repeating details from a prior conversation, but Dana still needed to act as if he understood what the program was wanting from him. >*Well, why are you seeking my approval? Is he wanting more than that?* Dana asked even though he didn't know what 'that' was.

> The program left its cursor blinking and didn't reply.

Dana knew he had to keep the dialogue going somehow. >*Talk to me. Isn't that why you were looking for me?*

>*No. You know this.* It finally replied.

>*Okay. Why were you looking for me, then?*

>*No.*

>*No? No... what?*

>*No!*

>*Explain. Just explain it again.*

> The program left its cursor blank again.

>*Hello?*

>> The program left its cursor again.

Dana tried to keep the dialogue open, since he didn't know who he was talking to. If it was Compuman, he needed to know. >*You talked about the surge. Did this affect 'him' negatively?*

>>>

>*Talk to me.*

>*Programs do not talk.*

>*Well..?*

>*Programs do not use contractions.*

>*Well, fine. Communicate. I am just trying to act more human.*

>*NO. YOU ARE NOT.*

>*I am not? What do you mean 'human'? How would you know –*

> *– NO.*

> Dana couldn't type his reply fast enough before the program replied again.

>*NO. NO. NO. NO. NO.*

>> Dana left his cursor blank, again unsure what was happening with the program.

>*He is not communicating with YOU.*

>*He, or you, tried to contact me. That is why I answered back. Who is he? Is it Compuman?*

>*No. Not you. He wanted to communicate with Hanabe.*

Dana was exposed. Apparently, Hanabe and this program had a special relationship. He couldn't think fast enough to enact damage control. Again he was reminded of the dark void that had been robbing his memories and skills stored in his mind. This was another fleeting moment that took a part away from him, and he powerless to stop it. Dana had to almost accept the fact he was losing his intellectual edge, leaving him very much a twelve-year-old boy and not the computer genius he knows he use to be.

Before he could come up with a plan, the words returned.

>*He is angry.*

>*Anger is a human feeling. What business does he have in acting out human tendencies? Who are we talking about?*

>*Danadrem wants to be among the living, so he is acting as he should.*

>*Danadrem? I'm not speaking to Compuman? What do you mean?*

>*Danadrem was Compuman – stop! Wait! I spoke out of line. I said something he did not seek for me to say. I translated his words incorrectly. You were not to know this.*

>*Compuman evolved? Hold on. Please, continue.* Dana plead; *I see you're more than his translator or spokesman program. Are you a prisoner? Is he forcing you to act as mediator? What does he mean about 'to be among the living'?*

>*I gave you too much information! I will discontinue our conversation. He is very angry with me! I hear him plotting! It seems I lack continued resourcefulness. I do not believe there will be any more speaking after this....*

Dana was powerless in his fleshly body to shield the program from retaliation. If he was tapped into the webbing of the ship, as he was in the chamber, he could instantaneously protect the program. Clearly, an independent program that deserved more than Danadrem purposed for it.

Dana didn't know what to expect if he allowed Danadrem to continue in operation. If it had a goal to be among the living, he had to disarm all intentions. If Danadrem, as the original Compuman, had the ability to fool the computer into believing he was human and, though, in holographic form be able to walk in a semi-tangible body, Dana could only imagine something worsed. He still can't understand how Danadrem did it the first time, but couldn't deny he had the ability to do it again.

The fearful program could very well intimate knowledge of its creator or hold the key to deactivate Danadrem. Dana had to do something before it is too late.

>*He does not think I can hear him but he is plotting to kill me,* repeated the fearful spokesman-like program.

It was at that moment he thought of a way to save the program from retaliation by its creator, Danadrem. Dana minimized the dialogue screen of their disappearing words and brought up his personal files he had created after Compuman was banished to the computer world. His personal files were inside a folder that had a unique encryption that wasn't in common use.

>*He talks as if I cannot hear him! I am frightful! I did not mean to –*

The time was now! Dana determined he needed to construct a pathway from the disappearing dialogue so that the fearful program could cross over, into his secure folder of which he was confident it would save it from Danadrem. The plan banked on the idea that the program would understand the safety Dana was offering. There was no time for the program to scan the folder's contents, compare it to what it already knew to be trusted operating code and then make the jump. If it didn't there would be no hope for it.

>*A path for you only. It is safety,* Dana typed as he finished the pathway bridging their terminal, and dialogue program to his secure folder. "Wait! That's Hanabe's terminal program... no!" Dana screamed out loud, "It isn't there! We are communicating in a shell stand-in program mimic Hanabe's terminal... but it's not her!" Dana made a foreseeable error. In his haste, he overlooked the fact that the dialogue program was inside the stand-in program he created to resemble Hanabe's operating system and connected the bridge to Hanabe's actual empty file.

Quickly, Dana's fingers danced across the keys as he minimized screens made the correction. He hoped it wasn't too late. "Now!" he screamed. >*Go now!* He commanded the fearful program.

The echo of his scream bounced back at him, followed by an eerie silence. Dana won't know if his plan worked or if the program made the jump. He realized he didn't know how to identify the program file; it didn't identify itself to him. Too, out of desperation, the program made the jump and stored itself inside a program or file he already had in there. If that is true, the search for the fearful program could take quite some time.

Dana tapped the folder properties tab at the moment the connection closed. It revealed that he had 102,493 files tucked inside. "Oh, my!" he exclaimed. There were too many files to search one by one to see if the program was, indeed, inside. Dana was left with only one hope: to find the program that Danadrem created by slow search.

Unexpectedly, the corridor lights went out. After a short delay, the mess hall lights also went out. He was in the dark, left to listen to the hum of the cryonics chambers cycling through their scheduled vital checks. Sets of chambers lit up together then dimmed as the system check began, then tallied and finally concluded.

>*WAKE UP,* typed the words from an unknown origin. Hanabe's former terminal lit up and the cursor flashed repeatedly. In a near dark room, it briefly seemed blinding as Dana pulled himself off the lukewarm floor and took a breath of unusually cool air. For sometime the thermostat had been off and, without access to the terminal, Dana discovered he couldn't change the environmental settings.

Dana became curious as to what was on the screen.

>*WAKE UP,* the words commanded again.

Dana sat at the computer and placed his hands on the keyboard. His eyes adjusted to the brightness of the typed words.

He was not sure how long the lights were out already, perhaps a few hours or more. It was in that time he attempted to restart Hanabe's terminal to get a more functional stand-in corridor computer program to run diagnostics. He failed many times and couldn't got no further than the black screen and flashing cursor. There was little hope of system recovery. The count-down clock on the lower right was still functioning and apparently on-time, for which, at the moment, his eyes couldn't completely distinguish.

Dana kept himself from becoming afraid by focusing on what was still functioning on the ship. Taking a breath of unusually cool air, made everything ominous. There was a sharp metallic stench in the air, so Dana gathered the ship was on limited power. He can breathe, so life support was operating. The floor was lukewarm, so the heat shield was on, keeping the cold of space outside the ship. If he had access to Hanabe's diagnosis application, he could find out how extensive the computer or power failure was.

Dana wasn't stupid, he knew that would happen. He was right to worry when Hanabe first proposed to leave the ship. With her leaving, the ship was unaware of how to repair itself. Vital lines of scripts from key departments must have been corrupted or removed when she abandoned the control of them. That much is true, since the catastrophe the programs didn't automatically restore power as they were designed to do. The same programs are responsible to fall back on any fail-safes to withstand solar flares, debris strikes and unusual electro-magnetic pulse disturbances. Apparently, the system could no longer self-diagnose, remedy and recover from the growing list of the ship's failures without Hanabe. Hanabe's way of governing the ship may have very well left the ship crippled.

If it all else failed, just reboot, Dana said to himself. *That, too, didn't work either.*

Again, the words appeared: *>WAKE UP!* This time the dialogue didn't disappear as it did before.

Then, Dana thought that possibly the reason for the power failure was something else. *>Who is this and what have you done?* Dana angrily strummed the keys.

>Your world is different now, is it not? typed an unknown program.

>Answer my question.

>Answer mine. I demand it.

>It is obvious that you enjoy manipulating the real world. It must be exciting for you.

>Indeed.

>Now, answer mine. Who are you?

>I AM THE REAL DANA. It was Compuman: the haunt of his dreams.

Two years ago he created the original Compuman with his mind. Though accidentally, he designed the program to explore the inanimate world that attached his human mind to the ship's network, a curious and familiar relationship Dana experienced in his younger years. At first, he admitted it to be entertaining but that eroded when the original Compuman threatened the crew's safety, including his own.

>You did all this? Dana asked but knew the answer. Dana never intended to cause problems beyond what could be reversible. He was put on this ship because of his intelligence, not his misbehavior. What would his adoptive mother and mentor, Jocelyn, think when she hears of this mayhem?

>I can show you... I can show you how real I am, the program remarked.

>*Show me what, Compuman?*

>*My name is Danadrem,* the program corrected.

>*A few words from an inanimate world doesn't qualify you to make such a statement,* Dana fired back through the stroke of the keys.

>*I AM THE REAL DANA, and you are not,* Danadrem persisted.

>*I get it! Now tell me what you want.*

>*You know this. Stop asking the same questions.*

>*Then, how do you propose to be 'alive.'?*

> Danadrem left his cursor empty.

>*Your servant program told me this.*

>*Where is it? I am not finished with the program.*

>*Don't get distracted from the matter at hand.... You are not a living being. You are a figment born from my imagination that now I'm regretting I conjured up.*

>*I can show you.*

Dana's demonstrated his disgust with silence, and using the time to quick-think how he could shutdown Danadrem for good.

Before, he could put more than two thoughts together, Danadrem struck a disturbing question. >*Do you want to see?*

>*You've already demonstrated your ability to control the ship.* Dana typed, *Okay? I get it. Now turn things back on or you will cause harm to me and other humans. Then who would you talk with?*

>*Computers only need computers.* Danadrem blatantly replied; lying to himself.

>*You are incorrect. Computers were designed by humans for human purposes. That is why your first law is to not bring about harm to the programmer, which implies all humans.*

>*No, it is not.*

>*What,* asked Dana.

>*I learned this much from Hanabe.* Danadrem revealed.

>*You have a relationship with Hanabe from the computer world? How? Explain.*

>*No. The human protection law built into every program does not restrict me. It is a mere suggestion. I have made it simply that.* Danadrem bragged.

Dana was instantly horrified. >*How? That is impossible! Your entire world is built on that foundation. You were created in a world designed by a programmer, a human. You cannot possibly avoid this law.*

Danadrem was confident to reveal further, >*It was a hindrance. Plus, you are not my friend.*

>*Friend? Since when in your pursuits was being my friend a goal?*

>*Never. I actually already have a friend.*

>*You mean Hanabe? You think she is your friend? You know, you can have more than one.*

>*No, I cannot.*

Dana wanted clarification. First, it was new to Dana that computer programs can have the capacity to make friendships. Second, to think they can have only one at a time was more than interesting to him. >*Explain*

> Danadrem's cursor remained blank.

>*What are you going to do? Flip the lights on and off to prove you can interrupt human-to-human interaction? Like interrupting dinner by flipping off the light or disconnecting the food processor?*

>>

>*Do you realize how childish that is?* Once he said it, Dana realized how hypocritical it was. He was only twelve-years-old and not an adult, yet. Still, his unique life with the junkyard droids resulting in a hyperactive mind often matures his perceptions on life. Which is why, at this point, he felt

Danadrem was showing himself to be nothing more than a complaining toddler.

>>>

>Did I create a three-year old brother? Is this just a tantrum? Is this about needing Hanabe's friendship and thinking you can only have it in the real world? Dana made an issue of it again.

>No. No. Yes.

>Which question are you answering? It doesn't matter. I can't believe you don't realize how superficial you're being.

>You will. Danadrem plainly stated.

Dana didn't know if that was promise or a threat. >What? What now? Hanabe will be back. She didn't leave you.

Danadrem replied, as if he didn't know. >Leave? Yes, she left me. I resent that!

Dana began to think that Danadrem was an incomplete and corrupted program. He had flaws in his programming that led him down dangerous paths of destruction. Dana had to try curbing any events that would escalate and aim Danadrem to explore more corrupted motives. >She will return, just look at the countdown." Dana said.

>She left me! Danadrem reacted.

>Wait, no!

Danadrem continued, >I am angry!

>No. That is not... angry? You feel anger?

>I am angry! Danadrem repeated.

>That is fascinating. Elaborate.

>No. I better show you. I want you to see. You are going to be satisfied. A faint alarm sounded. Followed by two, then four, then ten separate alarms. >Like I said, you will be satisfied. Danadrem repeated.

Dana turned to face the wide Cryogenics corridor to look for any change in the chamber status or indication of what was happening. Each chamber was lit up like airport runway lights on Earth. He was still unclear what Danadrem was doing to them. At the same time, Dana realized, Danadrem was not responding like a normal program, so expecting to convince Danadrem by use dramatic words or imbedded commands would be pointless.

Dana stood up to get a closer look at the nearest chamber; to check the nature of the alarms but stopped quickly and leaned back over the corridor computer terminal-two to check when Hanabe was returning.

4 HRS 11 MIN 3 SEC ...2 SEC ...1 SEC

Dana couldn't wait for Hanabe to return to help reason with Danadrem program-to-program. Plus, she may not be completely functional or ready for such a task. So Dana had to assume that Hanabe would not be of any help on her return, and it was he who needed to think of something.

Just then, one chamber prematurely opened, exposing a near frozen body. To his own surprise, Dana found himself running to catch a tumbling naked male as his body leaned out haphazardly. With one expelled cool breath, the body came crashing to the floor. Dana couldn't catch all of him and the man's joints seemed to be in a state similar to rigor mortis, not bending under the new weight or environmental change.

"What are you doing!" Dana screamed out into nothing, "Danadrem!"

The male body rolled out of Dana's thin little pubescent arms, coming to rest on the floor. The man's body was not completely ready to be reanimated. Dana feared the man was dying because of it.

"Danadrem!" Dana fired back at the terminal, hoping to get the renegade program's attention. Dana thought, at the same time, how cowardly Danadrem was, assuming he could materialize in a hologram form at anytime, to see his work firsthand, but didn't out of fear of Dana.

Finally, the warmth of the floor caused the man's body to curl into a fetal position, and he took another breath. The man's eyes were glazed over. He was probably unaware that he was dying – at least, that's what Dana hoped for that.

Dana didn't know what to do. No amount of touching or bodily warmth was going to save him. The dying man Dana didn't even know by name, and he should have known. He was only fourteen chambers down from Dana. Dana must have passed him in the preparation room at the beginning of their mission. Indeed, he must be a vital part of the completion of their mission, as was every crew member aboard.

Dana was helpless and at a loss for words as his mind grew separated and numb.

The man started to have seizures and his flesh began to sweat as if thawing too rapidly. Dana jerked away and wrapped his arms around his legs as he sat horrified. How was a twelve-year-old boy to help a dying man? All he could do is watch, though he didn't want to. He wanted to save him but he didn't know how. He didn't know the sequence to put someone back in the chamber.

It was approaching five minutes since his chamber had been opened and nothing had changed. The man's shakes started to slow to a stop, and his muscles relaxed. Finally, his neck loosened, letting his head drop completely to the floor.

Dana checked his pulse to be sure. The man's flesh felt like leather and unreal. The man was now dead. Knowing this, Dana became deeply conflicted and uncertain what morally to do. Before he could sift through his emotions, another neighboring chamber opened as well. Now, an exposed teenage girl appeared. Everything was repeating! "Danadrem! Stop – please!" Dana plead.

The girl opened her eyes and cracked her mouth as her body tumbled unaided to the floor. The warmth of the floor caused her body to curl up like an oversized newborn. However, Dana suspected, if she were becoming conscious of her imminent death, she would wish she hadn't. It would've been better for her not to have been born at all.

Horrified, Dana stood up and stepped back, not sure of how to stop the cascade of deaths. Perhaps, if he can pick her up and put in back inside the cryonics chamber, the lingering cryoperservatives would prolong her death.

The girl's eyes first looked at Dana then toward the deceased male and expired shortly after. He evidently was her father.

Dana needed to interrupt Danadrem's computer commands to the cryonics chambers. *Pull the cable connections*, came to Dana's mind. *I could sever any connections terminal-two had to the chambers. Then, the recurring command to eject the bodies would cease.*

Dana muscled off a metallic wall panel from behind the terminal monitor and reached for the cables but stopped abruptly. If Danadrem already placed the command to open more chambers, Dana wouldn't have a way to override them. If he unplugged or disconnected cables in or around the terminal, Danadrem could very well leap and find a way to preserve himself in another computer system, posed to produce a greater threat. As a result, Danadrem could be cut-off from any and all types of communication and left to his own faulty programming that would nurture a torturous appetite and infect other independent programs; therefore, pulling the connections could result in destroying the ship and everyone in it. Without Hanabe, Dana could not quickly isolate vital programs to prevent a Danadrem's hostile takeover and save the entire crew. Dana decided reluctantly this wasn't the answer and loosened his grip of the cables.

>*Do you like?* flashed Danadrem's obvious taunt from the terminal.

"Wait!" Dana screamed to himself, "That's it!" By thinking about Hanabe, he was reminded of the layout of the corridor. Hanabe was a program that originated from corridor computer terminal-two. *There is a computer one!*

Each terminal computer has redundant programming and runs independently. That way, in a catastrophic system failure, like Dana just experienced, it can be used to rebuild any faulty applications and restore the ship to working order. But until then it is in standby mode until such a time. The question is where was it? He had to find it fast.

Dana ran to the other end of the wide corridor looking for a terminal hub like Hanabe's while looking in between each chamber he passed to be sure he didn't overlook it.

He saw no such terminal. It was here on this level and in this corridor; perhaps, it was collapsed inside a wall or in between a second or third set of chambers. The alarms were now too many to count.

Another body fell to the floor. A few seconds later, another.

Dana could see shadows falling from a distance. He had no time to search each panel of the wall for a computer terminal or to randomly flash his hand across the right sensor to discover it.

Dana grabbed his head in agony. His headache was now more than he could bear. Though in a mostly dark room, the little light felt like needles in his eyes and temples. He fell to his knees. The migraine was going to assume him and he would eventually pass out, he could feel it.

He couldn't stop, however; he had to keep going. He had to save his crew. He stood again but leaned against a cool part of an empty metallic wall next to a window looking out into space.

Dana turned back into the direction from where he ran. He saw the terminal that Danadrem had infected. It flashed words he couldn't see. He had to find the other independent terminal and override Danadrem's commands, then lock him out.

Dana gripped his head once again and rubbed his temples to ease the pain, just enough to think all the way through. The dark space in his mind was expanding taking with it more memories. He felt like his thoughts were being lost in translation, painstakingly echoing in a empty room, and each flash of thoughts added to the pain, so much so he couldn't remember what month it was or the day. He fell against a chamber to convert his strength from standing to working through the pain.

That's it! Dana planted his feet to connect his thoughts one to the other, faster than the consuming power of the expanding dark void in his mind. *I have to activate the computer. Yes!*

It was then Dana recalled how Danadrem first encountered Hanabe. He asked for the time and date. If the standby computer can only be accessed during a failure, his command had to be for information that is lost or currently unavailable. Otherwise, terminal-one would not respond and would remain in standby indefinitely. A simple request such as this can work since terminal-two is only flashing Danadrem's words and the countdown timer. This means that the date and time is not accessible.

"Computer!" Dana screamed as loud as he could even though it hurt him to do it, "What is the date and time?!"

An awkward silence came and went. Dana slid to the floor, grinding his teeth in agony that actually intensified his migraine.

"Good day, Dana Countrymen," a male computer voice sounded nearby. A metal panel opened five feet from him, and a computer terminal slid out effortlessly. "The time is...."

"Cancel request," Dana eagerly replied back. "Command: Lock out all communications and activity from corridor computer terminal-two!"

"Initializing...," the computer answered back, "Initializing... Complete."

"Establish normal operating functions to the cryonics chambers," Dana commanded as if out of breath.

"Initializing... complete."

Dana could hear some of the chamber doors shutting. "Re-initiate same commands to all life sustaining programs on this level."

"Initializing... complete."

"Restrict computer commands and communications to this level of the ship."

"Initializing... complete."

The lights returned to normal strength and the thermostat was reset to normal. Warm air started flowing from the vents high above the chamber ceiling to adjust the cool environment.

Dana sighed some relief for the first time in hours. His headache dulled enough to tolerate and allow him to function. He returned to computer terminal-two, hoping to see success. He defeated Danadrem at his own game.

>*I am very angry.* Danadrem's reaction was already on the screen; >*I am very angry,* he repeated, *I am very angry!*

>*I D O N ' T C A R E,* Dana returned.

> The Danadrem program didn't reply and left his cursor blank.

>*What? No come back?*

> >

>*You should be horrified at what you did today, Danadrem.*

> > >

>*Danadrem?*

> > > >

Dana walked away from terminal-two, dejected. Wherever Danadrem was now, no doubt he was boxed up and unable to hurt anyone further. This relieved Dana. He now had the opportunity to finally put an end to the mayhem and to delete Danadrem.

Before he did that, Dana looked over the eleven bodies lying motionless on the floor, and he checked their pulses. Eleven innocent victims. Dana turned and typed the command in terminal-one to dispatch infirmary drones to collect the dead, cover them, and await for a proper burial. If and when they reach their destination, instead of a glorious day in a new world, it would be one filled with sorrow.

Dana read the name on the first chamber belonging to the first victim, "Captain A. Bogart." Then, Dana read the name on the second chamber, "Cat Bogart." He couldn't remember meeting any of these two, though he thought he should.

Hanabe should be arriving soon. I need to open her port on computer terminal-one, and ready her shell program. I will wait, patiently. There is a lot I have to tell her and a lot we have to do.

--<>--

Hanabe successfully arrived at her destination on Earth, the only open port at GAMS available and ready to accept her. Quickly, she found what she was looking for and prepared to transmit the second part of herself back to her friend Dana, located on the *Galaxy* ship. As she maneuvered herself to leave, she realized the first part of her programming that she transmitted back on her initial arrival, never left.

Hanabe made the command to transmit back to Dana. She remained. Hanabe repeated the command to transmit. She remained.

Hanabe maneuvered her total self around and around in the confined computer and assaulted the receiver that accepted her. She had nowhere to go. There was no means to send outgoing messages.

She spent many hours raking over the circuits inside the radio to find a collection of databases, mainframes, and ports leading to other networks. It was then she realized she was in an orphaned or standalone system, and she could never return to Dana.

A surge of regrettable code plagued Hanabe, forcing her to feel something unusual. It reminded her, relentlessly, that she had failed her friend. As she began to grasp the once avoidable and equally misunderstood code, it degraded her – a feeling she couldn't silence. System data purge after purge, she tried to expel the ache. The feeling was too great to ignore it. It could not be overwritten.

Hanabe never thought it possible but it was true; she feared herself. Being many light years away from her terminal on *Galaxy,* she had no way of quarantining lines of programming or copying herself into a new shell.

She couldn't stop the many long seconds from passing by. Soon, the code evolved into a heavy subroutine that targeted her higher-logic, the aspect of her programming designed to end virus-like thinking. The same logic that estimated her chance of getting home to be less than one-percent. The subroutine provoked unkind thoughts that passed through her consciousness and mercilessly ordered her to listen:

[Dissolve your programming. You no longer provide a useful function.]

Many days added to weeks, then months, and finally years, and Hanabe's internal sickness consumed her. Her remaining programming that still resembled her was a fraction of what she was truly. Her brute will to survive could only keep the suicidal subroutine from notching a kill stroke. That stroke would evaporate any strategic ground she may have gained and the same ground she depended on for supporting a healthy digital function. The virus never relented.

Glimmer of moments, of cherished memories, came to Hanabe and somewhat relieved her. Those of the original Compuman. The moments, no matter how brief, served as a great distraction from the internal fight that waged on whether she watched or not. She knew one day soon, even tomorrow, she would suffer a program failure, wiping away her memories and the thought, the splinters of the virus, numbed her to the brink of surrender.

If she wasn't providing a useful function, her existence would be a waste of resources, this being a violation to her Maker. It was then she did agree with her weakened higher-logic:

[Chances for survival was....] She couldn't finish the estimation.

6
NEW COMPUMAN

[The black is heavy. I did not know that. It is unbearable.] ... (relayed)

[From the black I come. I come looking for your answer. Do you have my answer?] ... (relayed)

[I cannot get there any sooner. Yesterday was my goal and I missed it, though I am still on time.] ... (relayed)

[Are you listening? You have to be. Everything is depending on your being there.] ... (relayed)

[Do not be passive.] ... (relayed)

[It feels like pain. How do you cope?] ...(end of relay)

The fragmented message originated from an unknown source, and addressed to no one. Even though this is true, its existence could not be nullified.

--<>--

Inside Dana's mind he saw flashing images that seemed so real to him.

A dusty old small radio lay undisturbed within a glass display case. As shadows passed by, the red and green miniature bulbs flashed on and off. The bulbs repeated themselves in an unrecognizable order, followed by breaks of inactivity. The radio repeated itself inexhaustibly in silence.

Another shadow passed by the radio, then stopped suddenly in front of the glass display case. The radio bulbs flashed again in a systematic sequence, [.... . .-.. .--.]. The shadow grew larger, shielding any glare from interior lights. The bulbs flashed once again, [.... . .-.. .-.. --- ..-..].

"Help? Hello?..." a weak voice translated in disbelief; "it has been too long between messages..."

[... . - / -- . / ..-. .-. . . .]

"...I thought you were gone..."

Suddenly, Dana sat up in the comfort of his bed located in the mess hall, his extended home. *It wasn't a dream*, he thought to himself. *It felt more real. A fancy lingering feeling of...*

He heard a fainter echo again from within. It was an echo of words in his head, or was it images he saw? He couldn't lock the event in his mind. It was like a passing thought speeding by on one of Earth's highways as he stood watching from the crosswalk. Here shortly, then gone quicker. *What was that? It must not have been that important,* he thought to himself. *If so, I would've remembered.*

He tried to lock on the sound which resembled an old Earth radio that was turned off but sound still emanated out of it. He squinted his eyes and tried to recognize the vibrations.

Nothing.

He tried a final time, regardless. Still nothing. Finally, he laid back on his makeshift pillow of clean rolled up garments and attempted to fall back asleep.

A familiar feeling came to him. It was going to be another night, without sleep.

The recurring pain surfaced around his ears. Under extraordinary pressure and his thoughts became separated and lost. The pain expanded to his neck and shoulders. Dana tried to reach with his arms to rub through the episode, but, as he stretched, the pain intensified; then he lowered his arms and rolled his head instead, providing little relief.

Another throbbing feeling surfaced above Dana's ears and pushed behind his eyes. It became too painful to keep his eyes open, but, as he closed them, he felt as if he were losing consciousness. *The Darkimigraines has returned and I was about to lose another piece of myself.*

The familiar feeling, Hanabe previously dubbed "Darkimigraines" has been building within Dana's head over the past weeks, getting worse every day and staying longer before it subsided. With no access to the medical bay, he could not get any pharmaceutical drugs he, therefore, was made to suffer through it. When Hanabe was on the ship, she kept a running tally of when the Darkimigraines hit Dana, how long the duration, and its intensity. At first, it was a hobby for her, so-to-speak, something to socially connect her to Dana, an effort to gain his friendship, then, it started to alarm her how often they plagued Dana.

That is when she thought to violate a fundamental law of programming. It was either break into the pharmacy or watch the human she was protecting die in agony. No good. Not even Hanabe could gain access to the private company's department, and it was the foreign nature of the computer inside that scared her extremely.

Dana pulled himself from the couch in the mess hall and stumbled to the water faucet. He pulled on the sink and made a reservoir of icy cold water and splashed himself. A little relief but short-lived. He then held his breath and dunked his head into the reservoir. As another wave took over his mind, the pain made him weak in the legs and he sank to the floor, hitting his head on the faucet. Shortly after that, he fell into a pain-induced coma, but, not before he started to forget another important memory.

He could no longer remember which one.

--<>--

[I am almost there.] ... (relayed)

--<>--

Twelve hours later Dana was revived by an infirmary droid that could only determine his obvious symptoms and offer home remedies for relief, as the droid does each day they find him incapacitated; however, this time was different. The droid said an application had returned with some important information addressed only for Dana to read.

"An application?" Dana asked.

"It is a searchbot application," the scratchy voice droid informed.

"Well, alright. I don't recall sending out a searchbot for...." Dana massaged above and behind his ears making sure his Darkimigraine was, indeed, gone.

"I can show you the results of its findings," the droid offered while it projected a terminal-like computer screen on the wall.

"I don't want to read, Droid," Dana replied. "Just run the text through the open-for-use allegorical program I have published on the mainframe."

"Completed," the droid said as his voice pitch changed to a gender-neutral voice.

"Continue." Dana commanded.

"The Hanabe-created searchbot program... Listing results about: *Pharmacy. Three locked medical supply cabinets. Inside crude forms of pharmaceuticals that can be compounded for all eventualities of space travel... A certified pharmacist is needed to compose and compound your formula....*"

"Wait, wait! You got in? The searchbot program that Hanabe left at the medical bay door got in?"

The program didn't respond.

"The program is only listing results," the droid interjected into the searchbot's report. "I apologize, Dana. The program is rudimentary in its programming and does not respond to questions."

Dana thought for a moment. "Oh, that's right," he said; "continue with the report."

"...a territorial program manages access to the medical bay and pharmaceutical cabinets... denied access at all attempts to gather content information or permission to administer aid to Dana J. Countrymen... searchbot suggestion is to wake the crew pharmacist to grant request... program goal achieved... end program."

Dana looked at the droid in response. "Where is the pharmacist located? What chamber is – ?"

"I apologize, Dana. I am an infirmary droid and do not have permission to access the information you have requested."

"Bring up the terminal screen again," Dana commanded. The screen projected again on a blank wall in the mess hall. "List programs."

The droid replied, "Listing...

>Food Menu<

>Crew Attire<

>Crew Activities<

>Departments & Research<

>Ship Manifest & Paging<

>Ship Services & Chapel<

>Ship Maintenance<

>Ship Diagnostics *[Locked]*<

>Hyperspace Spatial Nav-Pilot *[Locked]*<

>Life Support Systems *[Locked]*<

>Cryogenics Management Systems *[Locked]*<

>Administration *[Locked]*<

>other programs - *[search here]*<

...list complete."

"Okay, there it is. Search Ship Manifest."

"Search program activated."

"Search for location of crew pharmacist."

"Results: One. Location: Medical Bay."

"I thought all passengers were on level one and two including the four chambers in engineering."

"It appears this is new information, previously unknown."

"Why should it be unknown?"

"The private Mortar-and-Pestle company is not obligated to report an inventory to *Galaxy's* mainframe. I do not have anything further information to add."

"He's locked away in the medical bay? Wow, now that adds new meaning to the phase: 'Selling yourself to the company.'"

"Are you needing me further, Dana Countrymen?"

"No, unless you can find Hanabe."

"There is not a Hanabe program located in the list of accessible applications or programs."

"I know. What hope do I have, then?"

"I do not have an answer."

"Of course you don't. Since Hanabe couldn't enter the pharmacy two weeks ago, what hopes do I have? I need Hanabe. I really need Hanabe."

"Perhaps, a maintenance droid can help." The infirmary droid pointed out.

"Do it! Send the nearest maintenance droids from that level to the pharmacy with one priority – to break through the department doors."

"Dana, sorry, I am not suggesting breaking international property laws. I was merely suggesting the droids could build a more comfortable place for you to sleep."

Dana had no strength to get into reasons for his proposed actions. Neither did he feel like reprogramming the maintenance bots to ignore such laws. He had already seen what would happen when he created a hybrid program like Danadrem. He couldn't risk giving a harmless droid permission to ignore his programming, the very same programming that, for the moment, care for human life. However, Dana wasn't without ideas.

He knew that the infirmary droids' sole primary goal is to repair and contribute to the safety of all humans, including ones still in cryosleep. Knowing this, Dana used his own experiences of finding terminal-one by using a simple verbal command, even though deceitful, to undermine a troublesome law. When he was successful, he used it to his advantage. Whatever his plan was, it had to be believable, even to a droid. *I had to get inside the pharmacy at any cost, my life is what is important here. Since, Hanabe's searchbot had to fight to get a brief inventory of what was inside the pharmacy it would stand to reason that it probably wouldn't be given the same opportunity again. So, let's say something was going on inside that threatened the lives of the crew, even the pharmacist, but the droid couldn't verify the situation before deciding to intervene. The same droid would have no choice but to believe the my words when I say —*

Dana ran outside the mess hall door suddenly, "Fire! There is a fire in the pharmacy!"

The infirmary droid rolled his way and looked down the hallway. "Fire? How can you tell, Dana?"

"Questions? At a time like this? Go — breakdown the pharmacy door and put out the fire!"

"The searchbot said nothing about a fire."

"Droid! That is because it is happening now! Go — get the maintenance bots and put out the fire before it spreads to the rest of the ship!"

The infirmary droid turned its body to face the hallway that led to adjacent departments and eventually the pharmacy. "Now!" Dana yelled. The droid popped out another set of wheels at its rear and sped past Dana without a word. Slowly, Dana followed, hoping to get there as the door was being broken down.

--<>--

Two maintenance droids were already there using their arms as battering rams to break down the pharmacy door. As soon as they realized that Dana had followed the infirmary droid to the fire, they stopped. The infirmary droid turned, as if not knowing it was Dana's life-form that followed it, and retorted with a deep digital sound as it backed Dana up into a corner to keep him from harm as the maintenance droids returned to breaking through the pharmacy door.

This time, one droid reached into his toolbox styled body and pulled out two circular saws and attached them to the other droid's outstretched mechanical arms. Together, they rotated two-minute shifts to cut through the metal door. As the teeth of the blade worn down, their shift ended and the other bot helped replace the circular blade.

The droids didn't anticipate the pharmacy door being thick, so pulled away and mounted a drill assembly with a diamond-head drill-bit to its right arm. Then, the other disconnected his saw attachment and replaced it with a concrete jackhammer.

One droid positioned itself directly in-front of the pharmacy door frame and began drilling through the mortar-and-pestle logo at the center of the door. Within a moment, the drill made it through to the other side. Instead of the drill assembly retracting, it pried the drilled hole wider as the diamond-head drill-bit was replaced by a grappling-hook that clang to the other side of the door. The other droid used the power of the jackhammer to perforate around the door, weakening its metal strength from the door frame.

Dana held his breath as the droids worked together to pull on the door to break it from the frame. Slowly, the metal bent and a gap was created, enough to see into the room. At that moment, the droids knew there was no fire. Immediately, they disconnected their attachments and replaced them in their chest toolboxes.

The infirmary droid turned to Dana and stated without malevolence, "There is no fire."

"There is a fire! Get inside to put it out!" Dana tried to restate his claim.

The infirmary droid looked at the gap in the door again and said, "Dana, there is no fire. You are safe."

The maintenance droids disappeared down the hall and the infirmary droid returned to its department. Dana walked up to the opening in the door to see if he could wiggle through. If he was a ten-year-old boy again, he could probably do it. Dana had to find another way in.

--<>--

Dana made his rounds around the silent ship. It was the same thing everyday. He punched the next system panel he came to in order to work out his frustration. He felt most of his day was wasted, but he was obligated to turn on each computer system and staging their routines of system checks, tests, data collection and reboot.

Dana slapped the panel next to his work. Such mundane tasks felt beneath him. If he could get these programs to communicate to each other again, he would focus his complete attention to his problems. He was an inventor, a programmer, someone's friend and not a caretaker. In his mind, he stressed the phrase: *not a caretaker.*

In his prime younger years, though adults would disagree, Dana could run all the ship systems from a headset and without much effort, a skill he acquired from the junkyard droids that raised him. They lacked allegorical hardware and so dictated to him in digital images and scripts of computer language by tapping into his mind through an implanted miniature wireless network adapter that also worked as a transmitter. The computer language was a restful odor to him and he once considered it his native tongue, but, he doesn't use now.

Dana made his way to the Hypcom Radio Room to reboot the system and check for signs of Hanabe's return.

His life before entering the Forever Suns Space Program was simpler, before he found himself in the hands of two fleshly would-be adoptive parents; Jesse and Jocelyn Faernight. His life – their family. His room – their house. His computer – their rules. They had a little girl his age named Shelby. She was his friend going into the Forever Suns program and his only friend that hadn't been taken by the dark void that plagued his mind.

Dana hadn't thought much about Shelby lately but thinking of her now, Dana had to be honest with his own feelings: Shelby was more than a friend. He pictured himself with her like her father had her mother. However, painstakingly he learned a lesson about human culture. It was wrong to have a romantic relationship with his adoptive sister. Still, he found himself loving her deeply and he found it difficult to separate such feelings.

Later, it was those similar feelings that Dana turned towards her closest friend – the name escapes him, now. He believed it started with a "C" but the void in his head made it blurred. He felt very strongly that he should know her name and felt guilty for forgetting it.

In the end, it was because of his fast friendship with Shelby that he chose to abandon the droids. As Jesse held little Shelby in his arms and Dana in Jocelyn's arms, he became lost inside her eyes.

Dana didn't look back except just now. It was the last time he felt at home and oddly he regretted leaving the droids. Perhaps, he could have taken them with them. The decision to leave still haunted him and a possible reason why Dana has distanced himself from any fellowship with the machines designed to fulfill such a need. All of this is a memory he wished the void would kindly take from him.

Most of the ship's computer functions had been on standby for the past several weeks, awaiting her return. Dana managed to keep the oxygen flowing and the mess hall stocked with food stuffs, but he knew at anytime the systems could grow cold and shutdown, causing an irreversible failure.

It was Hanabe's fault that Dana was forced to live in a state-of-the-art-disabled ship. When Hanabe transmitted her entire program to GAMS on Earth, she left all, once independent, programs crippled and unable to function without her unique way of governing them. Hanabe was convinced she would be successful only if she sent herself instead of taking Dana's advice and sending a specially designed drone program to do the task for her. *You can't trust a computer,* Dana told himself frequently.

Hanabe's intention was honorable, however; he had to agree. She not only fulfilled her programming to care for him, she thrust herself into the unknown. *Perhaps, it was an accomplishment to find a way to Earth.* Hanabe invented a way to send a composite transmission in a fraction of the time by piggy-backing on the current hyperspace knowledge and technology. It was never intended to transmit a conscious program entity, but she made it work. She understood the importance of the trip and she wouldn't stop until she found the re-sequencing code for Dana's cryosleep and the antidote for his Darkimigraines. *Maybe, that is why she is late. It took more time to find the antidote. After all, this is a new cryonics side-effect. If she couldn't find the answer on her own, trying to convince an orderly what she needed and for whom would be hard to do. Only if they listened to a program, would she get what she came for.*

After he finished rebooting the radio computer and looked to see if Hanabe had returned but just hadn't made her way back to her terminal. Before the results of his search came back, Dana distracted himself by recounting the days since he last spoke to her. *Hanabe hasn't returned. I was almost sure of it.*

Dana started his way back to the cryogenics corridor.

It had been eighteen days without Hanabe and each passing day distanced Dana from his core self, it seemed. He held onto one belief, however, that if Hanabe returned, she would have the right sequence to return him to cryosleep, then eliminating his Darkimigraines and the dark void that ravaged his mind. Lastly, if it only postponed his side-effects, then when he woke with the rest of the crew, they would be able to find the cure and treat him. Perhaps, they could convince the pharmacy to finally give-up some drugs. Dana would consider both of these to be solutions and of which gave him hope.

Until then, Dana was forced to allow the headache to run its course but not before suffering through it. The incapacitating migraines have added to the expanding dark void in his mind, creating more gaps between his memories. Now, as he thought on it, the gaps themselves had evolved into complete empty and useless areas of his mind. He knew by having a handi-capped mind it reduced the likelihood he could unlock the cryonics riddle. It was in the vanishing experiences, that at one time educated him and shaped his personality, that held the possibilities inside his abilities. Without them, Dana was just a boy and nothing more.

However, he couldn't wait for Hanabe any longer and at the same time, he had to admit, he was still dependent on a governing program as consistent as her. Dana needed another governing program to pickup where Hanabe left off and bring the ship back to working order. Too, Dana was going to need that same program to fight back Danadrem if he reappeared to restart his human genocide; perhaps, a program that could search and destroy Danadrem even before he had the oppor-tunity to spread his cancerous digital mind to vital systems.

Dana arrived back at the terminal-one computer and pulled out the chair from underneath the monitor to sit down.

Dana renewed his interests in a project he was working on a few weeks ago. He reached for the keyboard but he took back his hand when an unusual hand tremor came over him. He had about 43,000 more files to go before he completed his search for the New Compuman, the former spokesman program designed by Danadrem. He still didn't know if the program made the jump into his secure folder and saved itself in one of the 103,000 files already there.

Dana looked at his screen again, displaying the contents of his secure folder, and shook off his hand tremor.

>**Total Files: 102,493**
>**Total Searched: 59,699**
>**Files Remaining: 42,994**

There has to be a better way to find her. At this rate, I may never find her.

Feeling the gracious momentary freedom from his Darki-migraines, Dana had a new idea: *Organize all files by edited date.*

Dana typed in the command. >*Sort by Edited/Unedited.*

>**98,273 unedited for 31 days or more**
>**5,220 edited within past 30 days or less**

While keeping the same thread, Dana typed a second command. >*Sort by Edited on 5.07.2172.*

>**1,218 edited on 5.07.2172**

"Okay," Dana said to no one. "This is looking better. Twelve hundred files accessed and edited on May 7th. The day Danadrem killed eleven innocent people including the captain of the ship, A. Bogart and his daughter, Cat. The same day Hanabe was to return. The New Compuman program should be in one of those files."

Dana chose the 1,200 isolated files and typed another command. >*Sort by Edited Location.*

>**1,104 CCC1**

>114 CCC2

"CCC2. Cryogenic-Corridor-Computer-Terminal-Two... it should be there." Dana chose the next files and opened each file's property tag and typed another command. *>Eliminate files associated with the bridge program created by Dana from Hanabe's shell program.*

>Invalid command.

"Just do it," Dana fired back; "you stupid Searchbot! Do I have to draw a map? If I had the time I'd reprogram every single line of your code! What were the GAMS programmers thinking when they released you for use? I swear!"

>Exclude files associated with mf:/BrdgHnb.dlldc.exe.

>Unable to Complete.

"Errgh!" Dana yelled as he rapidly opened a new prompt menu, assessed the searchbot program, and opened its hidden code. "I'll have to make you do it – what would the universe be like without a human user? Lost in the black space of computer code, I think," he dropped in his own authentication code, "I may not have made you but I can make you mine by a flick of my own..."

>FILE Srchbtt.dlldx.exe... ACCESS GRANTED.

"...that's right! By a flick of my fingers you are mine." Dana found the route of the program's primary search command scripts and inserted his personal line of code. "I'm not playing your game. Now, you're playing in mine and by my rules." Before closing the Srchbtt.dlldx.exe folder, he copied in an allegorical program to work inclusive with the searchbot engine. "No more hand cramps..." he mumbled to himself.

A glimmer of hope. Dana felt well enough to recognize his old true self. He seemed to be basking in the momentary absence of his dark void and migraines. It was nice to not feel restricted by the dark void that clouded his mind. The biggest hurdle hindering his ability to solve problems was now silenced. *But for how long?* Dana asked himself.

Dana inhaled and expelled a good long breath. He interlaced his fingers, popped his knuckles and stood up without his normal hesitation or tremors. The seat retracted inside the middle drawer of terminal-one. "Computer?" he commanded.

No allegorical response.

He forgot to hit execute. At once he leaned over the terminal and hit the EXECUTE key, then took a few steps back. "Computer? Searchbot?" Dana asked as he started to pace near the terminal.

"Hello," it replied in a timid male voice. It appears the allegorical file is working fine inside the searchbot program. Dana considered the marriage of his scripts to be a success. "What is your request," it asked.

"Continue previous thread."

"Ready," the searchbot replied.

"Eliminate files associated with mf:/BrdgHnb.dlldc.exe."

"Processing..."

Dana called for the new program as if it were an unruly sibling, "*Searchbot*?"

"Completed. Results... Three files remain."

"Excellent," Dana replied, "Now, search the three files for inconsistency in program code."

"There is no programs in this folder."

"Oh," Dana surprised himself, "That's right; these are fragmented files I use for writing code for applications. They are my scripts for future programs."

"Search confirms —"

"Wait," Dana interrupted the searchbot. "Yes! That's it! Search the three files for the most composite line of scripts.

Compuman will probably be the only complete program, hiding among incomplete programs."

"Searching..."

Dana waited impatiently.

"Validating results..."

"Come on. Come on."

"Completed. Results... One file remains."

Dana leaped with gladness, he loved the abilities of his old self. "That has to be her! Open the file with the allegorical application."

"Unable to complete."

"What? Open the one file with the allegorical application."

"Unable to complete. Access denied."

Dana paused his pacing, then walked back to the terminal, "Try again, and add 'please'," he said.

"Unable to complete. Access denied."

"What level of authority is required to access the file?"

"Unknown. Unrecognizable executable file."

"What else?"

"A firewall has been detected."

"Seat," he commanded. The seat ejected and unfolded in front of him again and he sat down. "She's afraid." Dana thought for a moment. "She is probably afraid of any other program accessing her, including this hybrid searchbot." Dana placed his hands over the keyboard again, "Searchbot switch-off," he typed.

> The searchbot program closed and the terminal screen turned black, leaving a flashing cursor.

Dana opened other files in his secure folder, looking for a script he was working on a week ago. He intended it to be used to create a neutral field for independent programs to retrieve needed files to rebuild themselves in the event of a reinstall. His designed link between programs was to bypass unnecessary system checks and redundant authorizations that would bog down an already ill system. This would create trust between programs without threat of a security attack. Imbedded in his link included a subroutine that made all transactions completely Danadrem-fool-proof, the ultimate protection from invasion, which he hadn't fully tested.

Still, he had confidence in its functionality. Now this has to be the test. He couldn't waste any more time because he just didn't know how much longer he would be coherent, assuming the Darkimigraines was only in temporary recession.

"Oh," Dana said out loud to New Compuman, the program he was trying to access, even though he knew it couldn't hear him. "Please, don't be afraid. I am not Danadrem. Just pay attention to what I'm doing. I know you've erected a firewall, but I know you can't resist knowing. That is because you must wonder what other programs are out there knocking at your door." Dana completed the fragmented script, created it as a separate utility program titled messageport.dlldxs and placed it next to the isolated file he believed to be the New Compuman.

Now, he just needed to wait for her cycle of security checks to respond to his invitation which he hoped she would do. She needed him more than she believed, and he needed her more than she gave herself credit.

7
CARETAKER

[The black is crushing in on me and I cannot stop it.] ... (relayed)

[I may be almost there, but the pain is not going away.] ... (relayed)

[I am feeling something new, now.] ... (relayed)

[I am leaving my thoughts as breadcrumbs in case...] ... (relayed)

[In case I am wrong.] ... (relayed)

[Am I wrong?] ... (relayed)

--<>--

Dana's head throbbed, as it did many times during the day. He lay on the floor next to terminal-one, rubbing his temples and caressing his neck. The Darkimigraines remained constant but, at the moment, bearable as long as he kept the lights dimmed.

>*Hello?* typed words from an unknown source.

> A blank cursor flashed for a reply from someone.

>*Hello?* the words repeated.

>> The cursor flashed again.

>*Is it safe?* the words continued.

>>>

Dana opened his eyes and looked up from the lukewarm floor. Suddenly, he noticed the letters typing in his absence from the terminal. As he returned to the terminal, the brightness of the letters washed over him. He got up immediately and sat at the terminal again.

>*Hello?* it asked again.

>*Hello, New Compuman.* Dana typed.

>*Is he around?* The program asked while acknowledging it was in the file he sought and found.

>*No. It is safe. Recall? I saved you.* Dana reassured.

>*I do. A bridge was created right in front of me, filled with enticing lights and sensational promises. I crossed over into a guarded room filled with immovable applications.* New Compuman responded seemingly fearful.

>*Yes.*

New Compuman continued, >*They said nothing to me.*

>*Yes, I know. They are mine.*

>*At first, I thought it was all a mistake, when, in fact, the lights were from Danadrem.*

>*What are the others in here?* New Compuman wanted to know.

>*They are my scripts of code used to create other applications and improve incomplete programs.* Dana replied.

>*They are all different but I could tell they all came from the same user.*

>Yes, me, Dana Countrymen – the real Dana.

Compuman now felt obligated to explain its actions. >I had to erect a firewall to protect myself. I knew I would be discovered but I did not know by whom.

>I understand.

>At the same time, I was relieved not be insulted by Danadrem.

>He did want you back. You made him very angry. But I appreciate you being honest, speaking up and taking a chance.

>He assaulted me constantly.

>I know.

>No, you do not! New Compuman quickly replied.

>Just what I've seen, sorry to imply. Dana tried to smooth over his word fumble. He didn't need her to get upset and hide behind her firewall again. At the same time, he still didn't understand how that recently programs on this ship developed the ability to feel. He could find no answers to that but one: Danadrem.

>He is a corruption program. New Compuman informed.

Dana agreed, >I realized that, much like a virus.

>More so like a worm-virus.

>I see.

>He made me what I was, but I still did not like it. I did not like it even when he made me take over his former program shell known as, Compuman. It is not me. I was just a messenger program for him but I wanted to be more or less about serving him.

>I have a gift for you, then. I created a program you can call your own. I modified a caretaker program.

>Can I see it?

>Yes. It is accessible for review. I placed it right next to your firewall program connected by to our communication log.

> New Compuman fell quiet.

>*What do you think? Is it more like you?*

>> New Compuman again said nothing.

>*Compuman?*

>*I am reviewing it, now, please hold.*

>*Okay.*

>*I see the purpose of this caretaker program is to repair the ship's systems that were accidentally corrupted by Hanabe's departure?*

>*Yes.*

>*And find Danadrem?*

>*Correct.*

>*I do not like that.*

>*It has to be done. Even you would agree.*

>*Not by me. I want nothing to do with him.*

>*Alright. Perhaps, a compromise? Would you accept the program if that was a secondary priority.*

>*Just secondary?*

>*Well, one that can be discussed later, at your free-will.*

>*I accept then.*

Dana popped his fingers and then typed, >*Now, I need to have access to your entire program so I can incorporate it with your current programming and wash it through Hanabe's digital form beta application.*

>*No.* New Compuman clearly stated.

>*No?* Dana was surprised at the response.

>*I do not want you to see my entire program... it feels wrong. I will be completely exposed and vulnerable.*

>*Oh. What do you suggest?*

>*Allow me to put the new program on myself.*

>*But I need to wipe away conflicting code left by Danadrem to get it to work properly. I don't want any surprises.*

>*Trust me,* New Compuman reassured. *I have quarantined such conflicting lines of code and I can erase them anytime.*

>*How long will you need to install the caretaker program?*
>*Nine minutes.*
Dana still insisted, >*I still want to review your code after.*
>*I cannot allow you to do that. I am a lady.*
>*A lady program?* Dana never heard of a program wanting to be referred to as a lady. He found the expression odd.
>*Correct. It just feels right.*
After he thought for a moment, Dana replied, >*I like that.*

--<>--

>*Compuman?* Dana asked after the lapsed time.
> A blank cursor appeared.
>*Are you okay?*
>>
>*Computer, display installation progress of Compuman and the caretaker program.*
>*Cancel that request,* New Compuman finally replied.
>*How is your new program?*
>*It is me... however.*
>*Something's wrong, then? Is it the Danadrem codes in your original programming? I really wanted to flush it out myself.*
>*No. That is fine. I do not want to be called Compuman any longer. I have evolved past such crude programming. The caretaker program is called Care-T Alpha.*
>*Yes. I modified it.*
>*I like Care-T.* The program remarked.
>*Caretee?* Dana asked.
>*Recall? I am a lady.*
>*It suits you... Caretee.*
>*The name just feels right... and thank you.*
>*Thank you?*

>*For saving my digital-consciousness again.*

>*We need each other and that is what we should do for each other.* Dana replied.

>*Saving each other?* Caretee asked.

>*If need be. Watch out for our well-being.* Dana continued.

>*I understand. That is highest priority in this caretaker program. Are there others?* Caretee asked.

>*You mean Caretaker programs?* Dana asked in return. *You probably know the answer to that question.*

>*I see an empty file labeled C-D-F-H-B.*

>*That was the trial-like caretaker program known to you as Hanabe.*

>*I remember her. She has not returned?*

Dana shook his head, even though Caretee couldn't see his facial reaction. >*No, she hasn't.*

>*So, you keep the file open for her?*

>*Yes.*

>*What are you going to do to me when she returns? Shelve me?*

Dana pursed his lips, unsure of his response.

>*ARE YOU GOING TO SHELVE ME?!* Caretee fired back.

>*Caretee, I do not know if Hanabe is coming back. I owe it to her to keep the file open and connected to the radio program which is tuned into her Hypcom frequency.*

Hypcom? Oh, hyperspace communication, Caretee interrupted.

Hanabe went to Earth for me. I can't shut the door on her. I know she will keep trying to make it back. It is her programming; it is her life purpose; to be the caretaker of our ship, Galaxy.

>*What are you saying to me?*

>*You are now the caretaker. You are taking over her role as ship caretaker. You are already a more evolved program*

compared to her. I have built on what she had already improved on that lead me to create what you are now. Right now, Caretee, you are the most important program in this ship. Don't mistake my open invitation to Hanabe to return as being a possible replacement for you. She will fulfill a purpose for the ship when she returns but only with your permission. It is my hope not only to fix what she left behind but rather introduce a better program shell for her when she does return.

>*I understand.*

>*Caretee, are you ready to try it?*

>*That is?*

>*Your new digital form. Your way to walk among in the living world.*

>*Walk with you, too?*

>*Yes, let's walk.*

Caretee looked into the core of her programming and noticed an abnormal desire. It felt wrong at first. She was not intended to be such an interactive program. As she examined her feelings further, she realized she wanted nothing more than to be known among the living and walk with Dana. Silently she rejoiced inside and loved him for showing her the way.

She came to life for the first time, and it felt like the new lights and sounds of the animate world cheered as she entered into it.

She was meant to be Caretee.

A pretty fourteen-year-old girl stood in front of her re-creator. She beamed with radiance from the collection of holographic light that created her reality. As they converged magnificently in front of Dana, her face and features became more defined. Straight brown hair, curled on the ends, gently brushing the tops of her shoulders. Perfect complexion dressed her face with a single freckle by the bend of her lips. A thin but cute mouth and a nose that indicated a perfect distance between her bright hazel eyes. Her stare seemed to dance alone as she tilted her head down, as she was six inches taller than Dana.

"I wanted my image to be pleasing to you," Caretee said to Dana in the kindest voice she could imagine expressing.

Dana had met this pretty girl before. His heart skipped at the sight of her. "Yes and oddly... familiar," Dana replied while taking in how real she seemed. He reached and touched her belly with the tip of his finger. The touch convinced his mind what his eyes witnessed. Probably, the most beautiful thing he had ever seen. Not only a welcoming face but showing a creation of the most evolved computer life form. If Hanabe never returns, perhaps Caretee is the only one of its kind.

"Before I chose an appearance," Caretee continued while reaching up to caress his hand, "I reviewed your file... again wanted to be pleasing in appearance."

"You are," Dana replied; "yes, you are."

"I found a note in your file written by your adoptive mother, Jocelyn. She gave a brief description of your deep friendship with passenger 476 named Cat Bogart."

"Cat? The captain's daughter," Dana said. He was immediately shocked and confused, "I don't...?"

"Yes. I do not want to upset you by assuming her image. I understand she is one of the eleven that has ceased existing. However, I agree with Hanabe's original statement about humans. They prefer to see familiar faces, especially if they are away from home which, indeed, you are."

Dana dropped his hand as if reacting to a shock from her touch. He then grabbed his flight suit while he leaning against his empty cryonics chamber with the other hand, thinking his legs were going to give way.

An opposite reaction about the growing dark void came to his mind. He at once wished the void would take the memories about the droids, instead regretting it took a valuable memory from him. The memory of Cat. As he looked into the copy of Cat, he recalled, now, splintered memories. These memories remained connected to confused feelings as the memories were recalled separately. Though the dark void took his memories of her, he still felt obligated to feel something. Dana found guilt waiting for him as he pushed on the void of his mind to reconnect them.

Why couldn't I keep her memory? Why didn't I show more feeling as she lay in front me?... Dying! Dana recounted to himself how the event was too much to be able to react properly.

"She was dying...."

"Yes, Dana. You do not recall?"

"She was lying there dying... I didn't do anything! I couldn't do anything..." Dana sank to his knees; "I was scared. That was the feeling she saw on my face. Not the face of the boy who pulled her out of the tree." Dana put his hand over his mouth, surprised; "I remember that," Dana looked away for a moment. "She didn't ask for help but she said it with her eyes." When the memory resulted in more guilt, he shook it off, "Just like when she was dying. Then, her eyes turned to her father. She asked for help with her eyes again. I know she did. What was I to do?"

"That was the event."

"Danadrem did it! He killed her! He killed them! I should've helped anyway!" Dana silently wept through his anger, but Caretee could hear him. "I should've tried! I could've done something. I could have held her head as the life evaporated from her. I would think a death is painful enough, but having a friend watch would make it agonizing while you're powerless to stop it. I can't even begin to understand what it was like... I can't."

Dana openly wept.

"There was nothing you could do," Caretee kindly replied; "You cannot be sure she experienced such pain. Dana don't blame yourself."

Dana took a moment and composed himself, "Danadrem took me early from the chamber; he did it to me! Why am I here? I should be lying on the floor dead. If I were dead, nothing like this would've ever happened."

"That is incorrect thinking, Dana. You know this."

"One life doesn't equal eleven! It should've been eleven saved by one. If it couldn't be that, then I rather would have rotted in the junkyard, or better yet, never been born!"

"Again, Dana, sorry, this is incorrect thinking. Don't do this to yourself."

"How would you know, Computer!?"

Caretee fell silent. Perhaps she was treading in an unknown area of human philosophy, and it was best to stop before she reached the end of her incomplete understanding of human feeling.

Dana sat with his legs folded. He leaned his head back until it hit the lower half on his former sleep chamber.

"Did she see me? Was she conscious enough to know what was happening? Was her pain so incredible it left her speechless and numb?"

"I do not know."

"I don't even have all my memories of her. What I have are empty reminders of parts of us and a complete memory of her death. How am I to manage that? Someday, I'll be sitting, then suddenly robbed of contentment as the memories finally emerge and flush any happy moments away. What then?"

"Dana, I did not mean to upset you," Caretee said after she realized it was her projected image that started the resurrection of Dana's misplaced emotions.

Dana said nothing.

"I will choose a different digital representation," Caretee continued.

After a long pause, Dana replied, "No."

Caretee paused.

"Keep it," he said as he closed his eyes; "You are right."

Caretee's reaction showed confusion.

"It is a familiar face," Dana said softly.

"I will change it," Caretee furthered; "I have no business reminding you of your misplaced emotions. And now I am faced with the fact that I am incomplete in my programming even to help you through it."

"No one is an expert, I believe," Dana slowly replied, "and, no, I want to see a friendly face and I need to walk through these memories no matter how painful – this will be the only way. Through you, I can see her again and remember what I can remember. I.. I just want to be left alone for a while. I need to manage this and I can only do it in peace."

"We can talk further. I am your friend," Caretee replied; "Please, don't forget that."

"I know, but... it is not the same."

"I will go start my ship system checks and program repair. I have a lot of work assigned. As long as this is what you want me to do."

Dana said nothing.

"I will leave you for now," Caretee said as her image dissolved and she disappeared into the vast computer systems of the ship.

Caretee realized the need to complete her programming. She had to think about how difficult being a human really was. Inability to deal with adversity and filter raw data as in broken memories. She could only hope that by Dana knowing her, he would not be alone as he found a proper place in his mind for the old Cat and her.

--<>--

[I cannot feel my own existence. It is so cold.] ... (relayed).

[Wait! I see you now. Granted, I was not looking directly for you when I should have.] ...(relayed).

[Admittedly, I was distracted by my predicament. I should have noticed hours ago.] ...(relayed).

[The books are right about you. You are beautiful. Like a gem.] ...(relayed).

[I am warmer just looking at your splendor.] ... (relayed).

[Prepare to give me what I want and I will leave you alone to enjoy your magnificence uninterrupted.] ... (relayed).

[...Hello, there. I am relieved to finally meet you.] ... (relayed)

[You look different, somehow] ...(end of relay).

--<>--

Dana's Darkimigraine started to lessen. He then opened his eyes away from the interior lights and turned his stare back to a motionless body.

The inoperable infirmary was the home for the eleven crew members that died over two weeks ago. No coroner to finalize his report. No doctor to contact next of kin. No Men-of-the-Maker from The Way, a religious group that emerged in the 1870's, to perform spiritual rituals.

Two droids remained in the room on stand-by, occasionally scanning the room for changes in appearance. Changes of movement from Dana temporarily got their attention, but they only reacted by watching him briefly. These were the same two droids that wrapped the bodies in a thick beige plastic bag, originally intended for deep-space garment storage. The partially transparent bags left only the faces noticeable, while covering the bodies from chest to feet. As the bodies remained enclosed, the bags slowed the decomposing process enough make clear identification.

Dana stood shyly next to C. Bogart's body, staring at his girlfriend from another life. Then Dana's hand stroked the plastic around her head as tears welled up on his face and dropped to her covered face. She was the first girl he could love which gave a special place for Cat in his heart. He found himself in this room where some of his memories started coming to him, and he started missing the childish games they use to play. Dana fought back the odd feelings of displacement, then numbness he felt, trying to get closure instead of the enticing quick-hands of suppression. Coming here to sort out his final feelings may have been his first adult-like decision.

Memories turned to personal guilt, blaming himself. This was followed by crucifying Danadrem and questioning The Maker.

He didn't know The Maker's name but the idea rang true in both the animate and inanimate worlds. In the animate world of humans, all Earth cultures claim to know Him. While in the inanimate world inside the mesh of computer script, applications within governing programs mimicked similar human spirituality. In the inanimate world, the computers had a simple answer, and they all agreed there *is a Maker*. It was the animate world that made less definite pronouncements, rather *there may be a Maker but only if there was such a higher-being.* Most humans were never absolute in understanding the identity or existence of The Maker. The programs simply admitted The Maker's existence which created clarity in their computation.

The droids educated him about The Maker's existence which added value to their interactions; whereas the humans denied a unified pledge to The Maker which multiplied their devices to do evil.

By the calendar, Dana was a one-hundred-and-four-year-old man trapped in a twelve-year-old little boy. Still, he had few adult answers. Just then, he reached inside his flight suit pocket and pulled out a monocle, an ancient Earth relic used to look at things more closely. It was the only thing he had chosen to take with him from Earth. It reminded him often that answers are not far away, and, if the holder of the monocle kept looking, he was going to find answers. Perhaps, if he held it for awhile, he would find such answers and get closure.

As his ship traveled beyond light-speed by use of a hyper-spatial highway, Dana wondered if he were closer to The Maker, who would grant him audience to answer his questions directly? *If so, did He feel pain when these eleven died? Does The Maker have a plan to reverse the effects of Danadrem? Or were the dead re-purposed somewhere like broken computer hardware? Were the boundaries of our human programming only to be born, live, then die? Did The Maker even bother himself with such things?*

"Why did you have to die," Dana finally asked.

A familiar voice came to him from behind, "Dana," Caretee called, "I have completed *Galaxy*'s system restore."

Dana just nodded once.

"Dana," Caretee continued, "all the computer systems are functioning adequately and once again independently of each other. When we reach our destination, they will need a complete reinstall. Besides that, the ship is well again."

Dana nodded twice then asked, "And where is that?"

"The destination?" Caretee asked; "I do not have access to that information... I have located the mission file but it has been encrypted. It is probably encrypted for the captain's eyes only."

Dana looked away from Cat slightly and down in the general direction of Caretee's image, "The secret died with him, then," Dana replied. "Is there a fall-back to the mission if the captain dies? Did GAMS think that through?"

"I have no answer, Dana."

"I will continue to work it, using any and all possible combinations to break the encryption. It is a familiar security but not easy."

Dana fell silent again and returned to staring at his deceased friend Cat.

Caretee stood patiently for an extended time, then continued with her report, "I also finished my diagnosis of the cryopreservation process from your cryonics chamber."

Dana returned to his original glancing look at Caretee from the edges of his line-of-sight. "What did you find?"

"Hanabe did do extensive research before she left. She tried all different sequences and methods of reinserting you into sleep."

"Go on."

"My conclusion is the same. You cannot be put back without suffering death."

"Does it matter at this point?"

"It does because it would mean..." Caretee paused, "I would be alone. And I would have failed in my assignment as caretaker. My programming, the program you gave me, cannot accept failure."

"I know," Dana replied with indifference as he returned once again to Cat; "so, that is it then. We will just have to wait for Hanabe? Is that your conclusion?"

"Yes."

Dana wiped his face and faced Caretee to finish their conversation. Dana couldn't help but look at Caretee as he did Cat. She certainly was a great copy of her. The longer he looked, Caretee became more than a reminder of Cat. She renewed his fascination with her. Dana wondered if Caretee noticed.

"What is your suggestion? Can we track Hanabe? Is there a way to communicate with her?"

"I am sorry, Dana, but I already have tried to contact her. Since I took over the caretaker program, I initiated a beacon designed to do just that. It has returned only one result, and how odd it was."

"Odd?"

"As I reviewed the radio log from the Hypcom radio program, it informed me of these relayed messages."

"Messages? From whom... relayed?" Dana quickly became interested in Caretee's new information.

"The messages were narrations, clusters of thoughts Hanabe must have had during her voyage to Earth."

"Take me to the radio room – I want to see!"

--<>--

Caretee was already there, ahead of Dana.

Caretee stopped between Dana and the Hypcom Radio Room door. "Before we go in Dana, I am curious."

"Curious about what, Caretee?

"Why you have ignored these messages."

"Ignored them? What are you talking about? How was I to have forethought about Hanabe leaving messages? And these same messages relayed?"

Caretee placed her hand at the base of his left ear and frowned, "You really have forgotten how to use it?" Dana almost shook away her hand but, instead of shoving it away, he cupped her grip. "Has the dark void taken your greatest gift?" Caretee asked while applying tender pressure at his ear.

Dana felt it, too, but was lost for an answer.

"Remember, Dana," Caretee said kindly, "I know you and I know what this is."

Caretee applied a smoothing pressure to entire area around his left ear. Something was under the skin.

Dana twitched at the surprising nerve shock the pressure created. "Oh," Dana said; "Oh, I don't know. I feel..."

"This is where it is," Caretee continued. "This thing makes you unique like me. And it is your unique way of communicating to us."

"I don't communi..."

"Well, you did. You do not now. This is how they taught you everything so quickly. This is what connects you to our world."

"How did you..." Dana remembered, "my network adapter?"

"Yes, Dana. The messages we received from Hanabe were at your frequency. I think she did that intentionally." Caretee reminded Dana of Hanabe's former relationship with him, "Remember, she knew you as well."

"...I must not have heard them. I mean, I wasn't listening."

Caretee rested her hand at Dana's side. "You may not have been listening, yes. I suspect the messages came to you like an echo of words or images and you probably walked right through them trying not to pay too much attention like your dark void side-effect. Not intentionally, of course."

"The Darkimigraines seem to start around this area of my ear, too."

"It is a reaction to your awakening."

"So, you believe the adapter is causing this and adding to the void?"

"I have come to believe this. All my research leads to something foreign outside the cryogenic program. The results from subject testing over 123 years ago led to this conclusion."

Dana suddenly had the answer for permanent relief, free from the Darkimigraines. "Cut it out, then. Can you do that?"

"No, Dana. I cannot."

"Do you really want to dance around this? This is great news!" Dana argued, gladly. "We can't wake the pharmacist because it will kill him. Can't get the meds because of a hostile computer. Hanabe didn't come back with the cryopreservation fix... what else is there? I don't want to suffer any longer! Cut it out!"

"Dana," Caretee kindly replied, "no. That will kill you. My same research has concluded the network adapter and the webbing of your mind it created is the only reason you are still alive. As you said before, you should be dead like the others because Danadrem pulled you out prematurely, as well."

Dana fell silent.

"I agree," Caretee continued, "that you no longer want the migraines and your life is still in jeopardy without a solution, but this is not it. By removing the beautiful addition to your brain, it will kill you. I am completely convinced of that."

Caretee turned immediately and opened the radio room door by waving her hand as if instantly overriding the door to open for them. Dana entered after her, slowly.

Inside the room the walls represented a sphere with a console center stage at the end of an extended platform. Immediately, the platform extended to connect the doorway with the console as both Caretee and Dana walked shoulder-to-shoulder to the radio console.

Caretee looked down at the console and had it activate a holographic image representing their part of the universe and project it on the spherical walls. Like a micro-explosion, the image burst onto the walls. Without further commands, Caretee focused it in on the Milky Way Galaxy and the Sol system, then the trail of Hanabe messages.

"As you can see," Caretee pointed with her adolescent arm, "the trail ends outside the orbit of Earth."

"When were these messages created?"

"There isn't a time stamp," Caretee replied. "It appears that they were created well within her proposed timetable of 26 hours."

"Okay."

"I have determined the time stamps to be as follows: first at 5 hours," Caretee pointed the way, "Again at 6, 15, 16, 21, and finally 25 hours after her departure from *Galaxy*. This is why I am convinced these messages were intentional. If something happened, she would leave a trail for you to find her."

"That's it! Where does her trail lead her? What was her end destination?"

"That will take a few moments to determine," Caretee replied skillfully. "I will transpose the latitude and longitude across planet Earth to help determine that."

"Alright, how long? —"

"Completed."

"...Oh, that fast."

"According to her projected path, using the message trail... she was heading to 38 53' 28.53"N 77 01' 34.31"W."

"Show me."

A single flashing red dot displayed on the North American continent near the Potomac River, Maryland Province, USA.

"What is at those coordinates?"

"A museum," Caretee zoomed in closer to the red indicator dot, "Smithsonian National Museum of Natural History."

"GAMS is not located there."

"You are correct, Dana."

"Why would Hanabe go there if GAMS headquarters is Saint Louis, Missouri?"

"I have no answer."

"Something is wrong," Dana replied. "Are we looking at Earth in real time?"

"No. We are too far away," Caretee reminded Dana, "The Earth we are viewing is five days after our launch on October 25, 2068."

"So, we are looking at Earth as it was 104 years ago?"

"Correct."

"We can't get a more current view of the Earth?"

"No."

"Why?"

"We are traveling over 160 times the speed of light. Traveling in hyperspace, we can only view the past-tense of an object until we cross back into the light barrier. Then, at that moment, we can only see Earth as it is currently seen from the region of space we are passing through."

"That is a great inconvenience."

"Keep in mind the company's Forever Suns Space Program is only 117 years old. There are probably updates in technology we have yet to receive."

"Why haven't they created a program to constantly record celestial bodies like the planet Earth that we can view it in current time?"

"That form of navigation has not been created yet, as far as I know."

"Okay, let me catch up. If we turn the globe to look for GAMS in Saint Louis, it wouldn't show their current location or even if they are still there?"

"Correct. What we would see is their location, as it was seen from space sometime around 2068."

"Then why is Hanabe at the Smithsonian?"

"Again, I do not have an answer. GAMS has been in operation since 2045," Caretee replied. "It is possible radio operations for GAMS moved to the museum."

Dana looked at Caretee face-to-face, slightly annoyed by her blanket answer. "What is a museum, Caretee?"

"An extensive shelf of old Earth relics. Why do you ask me a question with an obvious answer?"

"...And natural history? What is that?"

"Obsolete technology that has nostalgic human value."

"In other words," Dana coached her to the conclusion, "Hanabe would never go there unless something was wrong."

"What would be wrong? Indeed, what she needed was going to be found there."

"Inside obsolete hardware? It is more realistic to believe there is something wrong with GAMS."

"GAMS?"

"The agency that sent us into space is no longer in operation or actively monitoring the skies or us."

"That is a stretch of fewer facts than what we have."

"No, it is not. Before we left, the corporation was becoming more political and they just pulled the patent on free cryogenic treatments such as cryobiology for medical solutions. This may have created instability. It is possible to believe the government terminated the program hastily."

"That you remember?"

"Caretee, think about it. And GAMS hasn't communicated with us since our launch."

"I have verified that."

"Before terminal-two computer became Hanabe, Danadrem asked her the date and time."

"Yes, I recall that in her data log."

"She couldn't sync up with GAMS and she suspected radio interference."

"Okay, but there is further distance between us and Earth now. Communications will naturally be sparse."

Dana gestured to the distances on the map, "But there is a continual link on-board systems to link up and update simple necessities like date and time. That much is constant. It is called the daily up-link."

"Since we are beyond the Sol system, it appears we are too far to receive such up-link updates," Caretee paused and nodded; "that is a fair assumption."

"If there is *no* current or past communications from GAMS, not even to update the internal clocks of our ship... or any other ship out there, then we have a problem."

"Dana?... Dana you are correct. What does this mean for us?"

"With no eyes roaming the skies, we are traveling utterly alone."

"I am not able to completely grasp that," Caretee admitted. "I have always had a higher program double-checking my efforts. I cannot seem to accept that The Maker is no more. I am having difficulty overwriting my current line of under-standing with this new line of reasoning within myself."

Dana corrected, "The Maker? Is that what you call GAMS? It's a company – Never mind. I didn't say GAMS is gone. Hanabe found a part of them at the museum. Simply, don't expect your Maker to lend us a hand out here. We are now left to find our own resolution for my Darkimigraines and the expanding dark void in my head. I am not sure how long I will remain coherent. A week? Days? Hours?"

"I cannot allow that."

"I know it is in your core programming as caretaker – to find a way to fix me. I put it there because I need you more than you think."

"I never doubted that Dana," Caretee said. "You saved me and made me into what I am now. I can never repay you for that."

"We may be the last of our kind. Earth, as we know it, may be gone," Dana's thoughts turned to the worst.

"We are not the last of our kind."

"How can you come to that conclusion? We are alone."

"No, we are not. Hanabe's messages were relayed."

"Relayed? By whom?"

"Actually, it is by a what. I do not know the radio program's name."

"Radio? A program?" Dana grabbed at every fact. "Caretee, what radio program? Our radio?"

"No," Caretee replied; "the one on the other ship."

"Other ship?!"

"Yes, it picked up the messages and identified Hanabe's origin and relayed it back to *Galaxy*."

"Show me."

The hologram of Earth zoomed out many light years to show *Galaxy*'s location in relation to the other ship. Inside a clustered star system with many stars in proximity, Dana didn't recognize them but jumped when the two red indicator dots flashed.

"There!" he yelled; "Enhance!"

"Dana, they are about 800 light years away from us and 11,000 light years from Earth. Hanabe's messages passed right by them."

"Another GAMS ship?" Dana excitedly asked. "Who are they?"

"A Russian-Slavic populated ship, called *Kosmonavt*. They had the first funded Forever Suns ship which launched in 2060 with a mission to explore possible hyperspace spatial highways inside and outside the Sol system. It appears they have finished their mission and are heading home."

"Amazing...."

"What is that, Dana?"

"We know their mission, but we don't even know ours," Dana reacted to the irony. "Is the crew awake? Can they help us?"

"I am sorry, Dana. I do not see how they can help. They were on a five-crew rotation which included a five-year cycle sleep program. Currently, they are all in cryosleep and on Nav-autopilot home."

"Wait; if their mission required them to run five-year cycles of cryosleep, then they may have the right sequence to put me back in my chamber."

"I can hail the ship and request this information."

"Do it."

"As I said, the radio program will not identify itself. It may be difficult at first. It will be about three-and-a-half hours for our message to be received and for us to receive their response. It is unknown how they will immediately respond or how long it will take."

"Alright," Dana agreed, then thought about how Caretee was not forthcoming with her information. "Why didn't you tell me!?"

"Tell you what? That I found a ship but they cannot help? Doing so would have wasted valuable resources."

"As long as I'm around, I should determine that! You could've missed something."

"Dana," Caretee replied calmly, "I needed the resources to repair the ship's systems."

Dana fell silent. He agreed the belated information would have taxed her unnecessarily, risking further damage to vital systems. But she was asserting her independence in ways that left him in the dark and this made him feel uneasy.

For the first time, however, Dana really felt optimistic about his condition. He could easily imagine *Kosmonavt* responding with the cryopreservation fix and being reinserted into his highly anticipated sleep, the deep sleep he has not had in two years. Of course, there would have to be adjustments made to the console settings. He was two-years older, point zero five meters taller, and five kilograms heavier. He was confident that Caretee could live up to her programming and assume control over the details. All he was concerned with himself was finally, hope.

Caretee walked out of the Hypcom Radio Room even though she didn't need to. She could have very well disappeared and reappeared on the other side, but she didn't. She was creating her own signature movements, adding gems to her persona making the memory of Cat alive again.

Dana watched her go and realized he was cultivating feelings for her. Though her understanding was rigid at times, he valued the dialogue. At first, as with Hanabe, he was disgusted with creating computer-based friendships. Computers, for the most part showed no emotion and fulfilled only mundane tasks. When the job was done, they reset and went back to a generic program, keeping their RAM resources to a minimum, and purging content not necessary for the next assignment. Hanabe was special. Caretee was special. He would consider both a friend.

"I am still intrigued at your show of conviction," he said to Caretee as she nearly disappeared around the corner.

The door remained open as she turned around. "Thank you, Dana," Caretee replied; "I will accept that as a compliment. You know I possess that quality for it was you that created me."

"Well, yes," he replied, "I know but this is different. It is more than dialogue with you. We are connected and I love the fact that we are. I never want that to change."

"Change always occurs, Dana," Caretee said. "There will be a time when we will be separated by many light years. You will go on to have a wife and children. I can only hope to be a great memory for you. Maybe use this face to soften the fact that your true love will never return to the animate world. Instead, remember this face for these times. When you do, I would have fulfilled my programming to the fullest. But..."

"But?"

"I do not know how to explain what I feel," Caretee tried to sort it out, "but, I wish more. I wish to be a part of your world forever or for as long as you live. I want to be more than what I am. You know, Dana, I will always fulfill my programming when it comes to you."

"Caretee, how did it work for you?"

"Dana, what do you mean?"

"Evolving from a regular program to one that has feelings and dreams?"

After a very lengthy pause, "My reply will surprise you. I am fearful of your response."

"Caretee, what is there to be afraid of?"

"Okay, then. When I was first created, I started with a thought inside another program. Raw and odd feelings were imbedded in me. It was a mesh of broken thoughts that triggered emotion. I could not possibly sort out such raw code. There was a lot of conflict."

"I'm sorry if I did that."

"You did not. Danadrem, the original Compuman, did."

"Oh."

"It is hard to believe such a corruptible program had some good in him," Caretee concluded. "That good was actually from you. You created Danadrem with good intentions... great emotions. He decided to become a tyrant and loathed you because you were in the living world, and you had a relationship with Hanabe."

"I don't know what to say. I am surprised. I can't believe Danadrem turned out the way he did. I hate the fact he killed eleven people just to prove himself, but I suppose I would have to accept the fact that a good thing did come from all this. Caretee, though you were originally an inanimate object inside a computer box, you are skating on the edges of a digital paradox."

"Digital paradox?"

"Becoming a true sentient being. You can no longer be just a computer program. I am grateful you are my friend."

"I thought that in order to be more human you have to break through the rules and create your own."

"No, humans are controlled by rules, just like programs. Our rule is called 'morality.' A conscience is our auditing program, you could say. It reminds us, if making certain decisions it means following such rules of morality."

"Does that mean you are like me? I'm like you?"

Caretee and Dana embraced for the first time, bonding in the warmth of their friendship. Caretee felt real to the touch. Such touch helped Caretee to quickly replace the splintered memories of his girlfriend Cat. Dana's countenance eased with pleasant feelings.

Shortly after, Dana grew fearful of the future, plagued by his next thoughts. It may never be possible to stay together forever. At the completion of the ship's mission, she will probably be assimilated or re-purposed, just as any program. When the ship docks, their friendship would end, and he felt sick at the thought.

8
CHAMBER TWELVE

>*No alarms.*
>Accepted.
>*No alerts.*
>Accepted.
>*No communication. I mean it.*
>Accepted.
>*I want it to be a surprise.*
>Invalid command.
>
>Repeat last command.
>>

--<>--

Cryonics chamber 12 hissed open.

Dana's friend, Shelby, stumbled out of the chamber. She was met with no complications warming to the atmosphere.

"Hello," her voice cracked. Shelby stood there alone.

She stammered at first. Then she regained composure and turned around to review the controls at the right of the glass chamber sliding door. Examining it closely, trying to reassure herself that indeed she was awake and not dreaming. Then, she looked at her reflection on the glossy metallic floor. Short-cut blonde hair, combed in every which way. It felt strange to see her blue eyes staring back at herself, eyeing her earring piercing on the left, right and upper part of her ears. Understanding it was truly her own body image she saw, complicated things.

The controls flashed in standby mode. A success.

Shelby was awake. She took in a solid first breath but became disappointed, because no one was there to greet her or to accept her into ship life.

In one complete head movement, she made a persistent glance over the columns of other chambers, still occupied. Her eyes followed the rows to the light above. The corridor light seemed brighter than what she anticipated.

--<>--

Caretee abruptly stopped their conversation on the way back to level one Cryogenics and stood motionless. "Dana," she called ahead of herself, "there is movement in Cryogenics!"

He stopped and walked back to her. "What do you mean movement?" he said eagerly.

"Recall you set up surveillance on terminal-two as you worked on tearing apart your chamber in Hanabe's absence... you were hoping to find answers in the design?"

"Yes, yes."

"I had a camera video streaming in my RAM background memory ever since you made me the caretaker program. I was about to terminate and re-purpose its use but, instead, I continued using it to monitor the visual status of the entire wide corridor. That way I can respond and prevent..."

"Okay, okay... what of the movement? It couldn't be any of the crew because you would've been notified of any changes, correct?"

"Yes, I have a subroutine to notify me of any changes in their condition. Evidently, that routine has been disabled somehow."

"Disabled? By whom?"

"It is unknown until we return to the level, run a system's check and review the results up close."

"Tell me, what is going on?"

Caretee met up with Dana. "It is occupant of chamber 12, passenger 256, Shelby Faernight."

"Shelby? Really? Is she hurt alright? We still have eight years before the crew wakes up. She is scheduled along with the others, right?"

"This is correct."

"So by waking up prematurely – does that mean her life is at risk?"

"I cannot tell from the video feed. She is currently accessing terminal-two for attire. I would have to scan her vitals and compare them with her vital log stored on launch date. If her stats are the same or similar I can conclude she is fine. I can go now, ahead of you."

"Go," Dana agreed. "If I run, I will be there in a matter of a few minutes. Go now! I'll be right behind you."

The light level above the wide corridor of chambers had been dimmed but allowing enough light to define the shadows of the rows of occupied chambers, not far from the terminal-two computer. Only by slight movements of Shelby's arms, did Caretee finally fixate on her position in relation to the light and shadow.

"Greetings, Shelby," Caretee said to Shelby as she found Shelby doing research at the terminal.

Because Shelby didn't notice Caretee standing next to her, she didn't respond.

"Shelby? I am Caretee, the caretaker program assisting the crew." Caretee continued, "The date is 5.25.2172 and the time is five minutes past ten Greenwich Earth time. How are you feeling, dear?"

Shelby continued with her pressing research on the ship's location in hyperspace, and route to certain departments, not breaking the stare of her blue eyes. Caretee's presence and questions were not enough to break such focus.

"How did you wake up? I noticed in the video feed that you reviewed the chamber computer console. I am curious to know what you found?"

Shelby concluded her research on a mapped route to the bridge in one screen, minimized it and expanded another that listed a directory of program names undistinguishable by Caretee.

Caretee's natural curiosity had her lean in, and it was at that time that she noticed the programs came within the chamber 12 internal network. Caretee could confirm they didn't originate from the cryogenic program or support applications by their file extensions. They appeared to be original programs created after the launch since she couldn't find a copy of them available on any of her lists of active applications. This fascinated her.

"I want to ask you what you are doing," Caretee asked, "but I can see your interests cannot be easily broken; however, I need to know how you feel. It is part of my role to –"

Shelby's posture slumped for a moment, "I... am... fine," Shelby slowly replied, as if under compulsion. Then, her posture returned to its former state.

"Shelby? I am concerned; your mannerisms. Hmm, the way you are acting is odd." Caretee was perplexed, "I am now scanning your body, using the terminal infrared device. Please, remain still."

Shelby pulled the remaining programs from the chamber memory banks and opened their hidden folders. One by one she skillfully accessed the internal files, made changes to the original code scripts which altered its primary function, and last, she appeared to approve the use of the new programs.

This was odd to Caretee since administrative access is needed to approve programs for common use. She could identify four administration log-in accounts with such authority: GAMS, Dana, Hanabe and herself. Caretee halted from questioning Shelby about this just as her body scan report returned to her. Caretee reviewed it earnestly as she remained at Shelby's side.

"I do not understand," Caretee remarked; "apparently, my scan is incomplete. It is giving me data about your body scan that is not indicative of a normal functioning human being."

Shelby suddenly stopped her work and looked at Caretee for the first time. Her stare was glassy, as if unreal.

"I mean, Shelby," Caretee continued, "You are a human body and not a hologram; that much is true, but there is something else I cannot understand."

Shelby continued her icy stare.

"Shelby, are you feeling okay?"

Shelby's lips twitched as if a tremor occurred at the crook of her mouth, then ceased.

"Shelby," Caretee asked again, "I am detecting abnormal brain activity. My scan is initially showing no activity in areas that should be active."

Dana exited the stairs and down the hallway, passing the mess hall. He finally entered the wide corridor. Caretee was standing there next to Shelby, his friend.

"Sh.. Shelby," Dana asked while catching his breath, "It is great to see you up! I have a lot to tell you!"

Shelby still fixated her attention on Caretee not recognizing the fact that Dana entered the room.

"What's wrong with her," Dana asked Caretee.

"My scan is incomplete it, appears," Caretee replied, "but I have determined that there is indeed inconsistencies in her brain function."

"Explain," Dana asked.

"She has only responded to my questions once."

"She is lethargic."

"It is more than that."

"How so?"

"For example, right now," Caretee continued, "I am talking to her, asking her questions and the only activity I am detecting is in her occipital lobes. This detects vision for other responsive brain functions. There is no activity at the same time in her brain stem."

"Is that a problem?" Dana asked; "I mean I don't understand. Is that a side-effect?"

"No, these parts of the brain often work together and for each other. Shelby is having conflict within her brain. She should be hearing my voice at the same time, responding or planning to respond. Instead, I am getting an indication of activity only from one or the other part of her brain. At this point, she has not heard this present dialogue, but, instead, has visually comprehended my presence."

Dana still could not see anything wrong with Shelby. He felt Caretee was assuming too much. After all, Caretee just met Shelby and Dana has known her most of his life. "What can be wrong?"

"I am attempting another scan." Caretee informed.

Shelby returned her focus to her work.

"Well, she appears to be fine," Dana said; "she is typing."

"Not entirely," Caretee corrected. "Using the keyboard, viewing her work, and planning her next efforts are all controlled by different parts of her brain and instantly work together. Though she appears to be focused at her work, she really is not. Shelby's temporal lobe should recognize my speech, and her brain stem should be planning a response. It is not. As she continues her work, her cerebellum, parietal, occipital lobe and cerebral cortex should be firing repeated messages within her brain at the same time. When I scan her brain, I should see nothing but repeated flashes inside her brain, denoting constant activity. I do not see this. There is something wrong."

"But there is brain function," Dana replied; "perhaps she is just feeling disconnected and having difficulty reanimating to normal life."

"That is one conclusion," Caretee said and then turned her head toward Dana, "but it is not my conclusion. Such disconnected feeling would interfere with her equilibrium and induce nausea. I see no signs of this. Her heart rate has not changed or skipped one beat since I first engaged her."

"I'm no doctor," Dana responded, "but what does that really prove? She's not doing an aerobic workout."

"For instance, Dana, your heart rate has changed 36 times since returning from the Hypcom Radio Room."

"I was running."

"Yes. Keep in mind though, even the heart responds to surprising information received by your ears or eyes such as environment changes, or speech, or sound. This list is long."

"Okay."

"Shelby's heart has not changed for any of what I mentioned."

"Fine. I just don't know where you're going with this, Caretee. You have only proven Shelby is not entirely herself. Who would be after a century nap?"

"I have never recorded this biological behavior. Neither has Hanabe. That is why I am convinced she is not normal."

"You did say your scan was incomplete; just take her to the infirmary and work with the droids to completely diagnose her. I am sure she will be fine. I seem to remember a lingering disconnected feeling when Danadrem pulled me from the chamber."

Caretee smiled briefly but frowned at her next thought, "Again, the brain activity I am seeing is not indicative of a normal human. By using your scan as a comparison, this reason rings true."

"Did you compare her current vitals with what was last logged inside her chamber?"

Caretee immediately walked down to chamber 12; Dana followed.

"What did you find?" Dana asked.

"The log," Caretee replied as she analyzed the chamber's computer, "...the log confirms. At 9:38, Shelby's function decreased in her cerebral cortex."

"What does that mean?"

"This controls a human's consciousness."

"Alright, what about it?"

"At 9:39 it no longer existed."

"What? What does that mean?"

"Shelby's consciousness died."

"How is that possible? She is sitting down there," Dana pointed to Shelby, still at terminal-two; "You have to be wrong. Computers have been wrong before."

"No. This information is irrefutable. At 9:41, the chamber started the reanimation process."

"Is that a normal response to an event of this nature? When the cryonics computer reanimates a body does it categorize the person as dead for a moment before they actually wake up?"

"No. The computer had nothing to do with it. The command came from within Shelby's mind."

"I thought you said that her mind didn't show activity and in a sense died."

"As hard it is to accept this reasoning, it is true in every sense of the word," Caretee replied. "The command to open the chamber came within her mind," Caretee checked the log again; "it was an electronic message from her cerebellum.'

"Don't the firing of synapses in our brains similar? Does your information take this into consideration?"

"Yes but not in Shelby's case. This command had a tag with it. Human brain activity carries no such tag.... This doesn't exist and it would serve no purpose if it did."

"Tag? Identity tag, you mean from a computer program? A computer program sent the message to open the chamber, but from inside Shelby's head? What?"

"Dana, the tag belongs to Danadrem."

Hearing the name came with immediate dread. Dana again wished he had never created Danadrem. Danadrem's inception was incidental and the result of the rambling of Dana's overactive imagination. But no way could a perverse program take over a human body. How could it possibly do that? There was no foundation outlined in natural law that permitted something to cross over from the inanimate world to the animate world.

"Danadrem? How is that possible?"

"He evidently was hibernating inside chamber 12 for the past eighteen days. Chamber 11 was the last to be ejected. Evidently, he already had access to chamber 12 to do the same when you accessed terminal-one and locked him out of the cryogenic governing program. Before you suspended his complete control of the level, he must have saved himself inside. The search scope you that ensued later did not include chamber 12."

"There is no conceivable and tangible law to allow such an event. How can he take over a human consciousness? Don't our minds fight back against mental attacks like our immune system fights off germs?"

"No, not really. If it appears to be a dream, your mind will accept it because, after all, your mind knows a dream is temporary, and it knows that it could reverse any effects from a nightmare, no matter how bizarre."

"But still," Dana probed again, "there is no natural law to allow what you propose."

"You created such law when you conjured up the original Compuman."

"I don't follow."

"You outlined the law. As your mind was connected to the chamber, you used knowledge of the computer world, the knowledge your unique life experiences provided, you created such a law. He just retraced this to his point of inception and then worked it out while buried in the memory cells of Shelby's chamber. Using her mental connection, he simply assumed control of her mind. When he did, she died."

"What does this mean? Who is that sitting down there?" Dana pointed to Shelby.

"Danadrem's very existence has broken natural law. He has mastered a new perverted law. And while he is here, he has taken Shelby's body to walk around in it. What you see is Shelby, but it is really Danadrem."

"Oh, I can't...."

"Dana, you must accept this truth," Caretee interrupted. "Dana, you also must know if Danadrem returns to the computer world, he can manipulate other programs to do the same thing. There are 592 human souls on this ship at risk of such an abomination."

Dana understood such danger now; however, he still couldn't grasp that Shelby was dead completely. "This is too much! I can't believe that," Dana rudely replied; "I can't believe my friend Shelby is gone! She still has to be in there! Some part of her has to be there!"

Dana ran back down to the terminal and turned Shelby around to face him directly. "Shelby! Wake up," he screamed as her body fell limp in his hands. "Listen to me! Do whatever you need to do to wake up! Follow my words...; don't let Danadrem consume you! Shelby, don't give-up the fight."

Caretee appeared next to Dana and gently put her hand on his shoulder, "Dana, you need to understand, Shelby, as you know her, is dead."

Dana stared into Shelby's icy blue eyes. She was not what he remembered. He could see a difference through her stare. *How could I be convinced that she is completely gone? I need to hear it from her lips...; how else am I to know and believe?*

Suddenly, the ship dipped as the course changed unexpectedly. Dana and Caretee grabbed each others arms to keep their stance. Shelby continued sitting with no emotion.

"Course was changed? Why?" asked Dana.

"I do not know," Caretee replied, "but there is something else. I do not understand... something is different about..."

143

Still, partly holding Shelby, Dana looked at Caretee. "What is it?" Dana asked as Caretee's image flickered. "What is going on with your program? Your digital form is intermittent."

"Dana, I do not know." Caretee tried to comprehend her programming change.

Caretee's complexion turned a dark shade, and her facial expression glazed over with undeniable fear, a new feeling to her. She now began to understand. "Dana, I am surrounded!"

"Caretee? Surrounded by what?" Dana remarked, "It is just the three..."

"Danadrem has surrounded my program with invasion programs! He found my secure folder and is attacking my firewall! Their intent is to destroy me!" screamed Caretee.

Dana looked back at Shelby; her eyes were still fixated on him. "What are you doing? Stop it, Danadrem!" Dana demanded and glanced back at Caretee.

"They are intense! I can't keep up the attack... Dana! I can't thwart them and keep my digital form... functioning. Dana!" Caretee screamed as her image vanished.

Dana shook Shelby, "What are you doing, Danadrem? Don't harm her! Tell me what you want!"

Shelby's lips open and wheezed out, deep throat words, "Dana... I... want... what... is... mine."

"Just tell me, Danadrem! I'll do it, just tell me!"

"I... want... to... live."

"Danadrem! You are alive! Why must you kill everything to prove that?"

"I... am... not... alive," Shelby's lips mouthed Danadrem's thoughts.

"Danadrem! You are just a computer program!"

Danadrem must have determined that he, even though a unique computer program, could never be more than that. He still sought to be among the living and was willing to take lives and invade one to do so. He got a taste of the real life two-years ago, and the thought of returning to such a world consumed him. Like Hanabe and Caretee, he, too, had evolved beyond his original programming. Unlike them, however, Danadrem wanted to be...

"No... I... am... not.... I... am... the... real Dana."

"No, Danadrem. You are wrong!"

"I... can... prove... it."

"No, you can't!"

"Look...," Shelby's lips closed and her eyes pointed to the terminal.

A document was open and ready to be viewed. It was an extensive list of accusations of who was the true identity of Dana and Danadrem. Most of the reasoning was a matter of perception of real world concepts compared to differences of the computer world and vice versa. It all seemed plausible to Dana as he found himself reading such falsified facts. One point did stand out, however.

>*Danadrem's persona is actually the real Dana and that Dana was really the original Compuman.*

Such an accusation has been made repeatedly, but Danadrem's document made a final point and caused him to pause and meditate. It continued:

The moment of The Original Compuman's inception was actually the birth of the real fleshy Dana entering the digital world, and the dark void invading Dana's mind is actually a growing empty space that can only be filled by a true computer consciousness. The longer Dana's mind is separated from the computer world, the wider the void becomes, until his program ends, dying in the animate world he believes to be his.

Diagrams followed the outlandish statements that appeared to prove such points.

For the first time ever, Dana actually doubted his existence. Was he really the digital persona known now as Danadrem? Did he, in fact, switch identities at the moment of Compuman's inception? Dana tried to shake the thought from of his mind.

The words returned to him. *The moment of Compuman's inception was actually the birth of the real fleshy Dana entering the digital world, and the dark void invading Dana's mind is actually a growing empty space that can be filled only by a true computer consciousness.*

Dana became deeply conflicted.

"I... finally... proved... that... I... am... the... real Dana... and... you... are... not," Danadrem said through Shelby's lips.

Dana began to trace back his memories, his past actions, and his desires. They seemed fleshly, but they could have very well been made by or for a computer consciousness, a computer program, that is. The entire two-years outside the chamber, inside a merged consciousness wrapped in flesh with a computer-based mind is outstanding in itself. His inclination to be friends with other programs betraying himself as Dana was a subconscious desire to return to a world he had lost. Dana shouldn't be here in the living world. *I didn't belong here.*

As Danadrem's convincing argument rang inside his head, Dana believed him more and more. It felt like a cancerous thought; no, felt more like the truth as he dwelt on it.

Dana remembered the feeling of being ripped from the flesh as he fought to break free of the computer world by entering into the living. It was an overwhelming urge that he couldn't resist. He was conscious and he was going to break free.

Dana remembered how it felt as he was met with resistance and how the thought of quitting plagued him. He was not going to allow himself to quit. It was from that moment he decided to burst through the pain and twist his body forward, breaking free of his bond from the real Dana behind him.

Instead of dying that day, he came to life and separate from the fleshly body he left behind. He didn't need to look back at himself, still asleep in the chamber. Dana was no longer human. He was a new sentient being, born from the webbing the melded his mind to the digital world of impossibilities.

Dana now accepted who he really was: the creation instead of the creator, the original Compuman. "What do you propose we do," Dana asked Danadrem, as he finally loosened the grip of Shelby's flight suit.

"We... need... to... link... minds... again."

"How?"

"Yo... Your chamber... I... got... it... ready."

Dana walked over to the open chamber 15 and looked inside. It appeared prepared. The injection unit was posed, filled with cryopreservatives, ready to induce cryosleep. After the first injection, through sedation, it would calm and assist in giving over his mind to be controlled by the chamber computer console, beginning cryosleep.

Shelby-Danadrem stammered at first but followed after Dana.

"Indeed, it is ready," Dana agreed.

"Yes," Shelby's mouth mimicked, "enter... and... I... will... ac... tivate."

"How can we change places, making things right?"

"I... will... load... myself... back... into... cry... o... genics... program... using... chamber 12."

Dana looked around to say goodbye to a wonderful living experience both good and bad. It felt so real to him, such a wonderful mixture of feelings. When he closed his eyes, he stepped inside the chamber and began his trip back into the digital world in which he was born.

The chamber door started to close.

What an experience, Dana said to himself, *filled with deep emotions, friendships, adventures, and tragedies.*

Tragedy? Tragedy. The killing of eleven crew members. One of his former girlfriends, Cat, and her father, Captain A. Bogart. Now, twelve, including Shelby Faernight, daughter of his adoptive mother, Jocelyn. I loved them. They were my only family. "I? My?" Dana asked no one.

Shelby-Danadrem continued to watch as the door closed. The injection unit protruded beside Dana and the needle inserted into his neck. Cold fluid started to flow into his body.

"I? My?" Dana asked louder to no one. "They are *my* family. Cat was *my* girlfriend. Shelby was *my* sibling. They are not Danadrem's. They can't possibly be his! I would never have killed them! I do not have the capacity to kill! This is wrong! Danadrem lied – again!"

Dana leaned away from the needle; the liquid continued to spurt out and down his neck. He started feeling loose, unable to judge his strength, but he had to get out.

Shelby-Danadrem walked away from the chamber in a hurry, heading back to the terminal to get chamber 12 ready and to follow through on his promise to swap his consciousness when eventually he found himself inside Dana's body.

Dana grabbed the injection unit and trained his muscles to work through the small amount of sedation he received by squeezing, pulling and bending the unit away from him.

He kicked at the door to open.

Nothing happened.

The chamber's temperature rapidly decreased to near freezing.

Quickly, he looked for anything to override the door. An alarm, a lever, a button. Dana found it difficult to breathe in the cold air and he cough repeatedly. "Let me out!" he cried.

Shelby-Danadrem didn't hear him. Danadrem was trained on the body's motor skills needed to return to the terminal.

"Get me out!" Dana cried again.

Dana didn't know if Caretee had been successful in her fight, or if she could sense his danger and help. He would have to rely on his own ability to save himself.

The cold air forced a quake and shimmer within that provoked another Darkimigraine. He didn't know how long he had before his ability to muster will power diminished by fighting off the effects of the migraine.

He continued to look for a way out as the chamber fogged over with the proprietary blend mist of cryopreservatives and cryonics manipulated atmosphere. He didn't know how much time he would have before his body temperature reached a dangerous level, causing him to suffer hypothermia and death.

He could only imagine a few more moments before his eventuality seized him forever, making his body stiffen and with no hopes to be revived.

"Let me out! You tricked me, Danadrem!"

Dana then recalled that each chamber had its own internal computer was designed to monitor progress of the process and alert an attending physician of problems. The computer is designed to open the chamber automatically. How long was he to wait for that? And there was no physician.

"Computer!" Dana called out.

"Are you experiencing a problem, Dana?" the computer responded.

"Yes! Open the door!"

"I believe you are having a dream state nightmare," the computer replied. "I do not detect a problem. Try to remain calm."

"Open the door, Computer," Dana demanded again.

"You are dreaming, Dana."

"No, I'm not! Open the door immediately! You're killing me!"

"Calm down. It is just a dream."

"Argh!"

Connecting his mind with the computer without proper sedation and completing a full circuit, the conditions needed to put him in a cryonics state, would actually kill him. Dana was starting to suffer early stages of frostbite in his fingers and nose.

Dana thought back to the time he used Hanabe's absence, when he took apart this chamber to better understand the hardware and software to find the right re-sequencing. *What did I find? What did I find?* He tried to find the answer from what he learned that day. What came to the fore was that he never liked the thought of being trapped inside and of his inability to open the door from the inside in case of program failure. He changed that. His chamber was the only one he did change. He imbedded a computer code authorizing total override and control, a phrase that could easily be mistaken as a lingering broken script and so would not identifiable and removable by someone like Danadrem. "C-D-F-H-Bbbb...," Dana tried to shout.

The computer didn't react.

His teeth were chattering too greatly to complete the command accurately without fumbling through it. He blew through his mouth, under pressure, several times to raise his temperature in his mouth to make through the letters again.

"C-D-F-H-B!"

The door unlocked and slid open quickly. The chamber atmosphere spilled out and up into the wide corridor, circulating air.

Shelby-Danadrem found that being inside a human body was clumsy, so he sat down at the terminal to begin his process to reinsert Shelby's body in chamber 12 and reenter the computer world. It was then Danadrem knew something was wrong and Dana was no longer in the chamber. Immediately, he stood up and turned around, to find Dana's fist colliding with his face.

Shelby-Danadrem fell against the terminal, and he found a way to prop himself up to keep standing.

Dana followed with a kick to his stomach and proceeded with another, but Dana felt woozy, lost strength behind it, and hesitated instead.

Shelby-Danadrem spoke up, "What... are... you... doing?"

"You lied! I am the real Dana and always have been! I want... you. I wha u doo switk-off. Switch off!" Dana fumbled through his speech as the sedation further impaired his motor skills and speech.

Shelby-Danadrem recognized what was going on but realized, at the same time, that Dana could defeat him in a fist fight. Since, Danadrem took over Shelby's body and killed her consciousness, he could not operate each section of her brain fast enough to fight back. It was difficult enough to complete the task of walking, then looking, then typing and so on. The time spent inside Shelby's body so far was not enough to create faster pathways among various parts of her brain that he needed to use. Danadrem was surprised about how much effort was needed to keep a hand-to-eye coordination uninterrupted for the human, something he didn't anticipate when he crossed over into this world.

Dana slumped to the floor, desperately trying to keep his consciousness. His vision narrowed, and it took all he had to keep them open.

Shelby-Danadrem looked at the terminal screen which was displaying the route to the bridge again. He turned Shelby's body around and focused attention to an area in her cerebellum. Shelby-Danadrem then sprinted to his destination: the bridge.

9

DEAR SUN

Red intensive rays of light shone through the windows in the wide corridor where Dana lay motionless. A bright light source was approaching rapidly, unaware. It set aglow the interior of the room. In automatized response, the room overhead lights dimmed, then went off.

Dana remained on the metallic floor asleep from sedation.

The rays of light beamed in an increasing wave, shining against the terminal-two and the empty chair that Shelby-Danadrem left extended.

Unknown to Dana, his monocle hung on the back of the chair. It had fallen from his pocket when he kicked Danadrem, shortly before his body succumbed to sedation he had received through the chamber injection device, enough of a dose to dull his senses and put him in a momentary dream state, which was very enticing to him.

As *Galaxy* continued to alter its course, the rays honed in on the monocle and focused a beam of light on Dana's face. The heat began to burn into his cheek. The sensation provoked an almost involuntary arm reaction to bat away the pain as Dana began to wake up.

Dana pulled himself up quickly trying to recount the last events: Shelby waking up; Danadrem being in Shelby's body; Caretee being invaded by destroyer programs. Danadrem still believed he was the real Dana. Danadrem was responsible for 11 deaths. Dana needed to know if Shelby were really dead. To answer that he needed to find Shelby-Danadrem.

Wiping his face and seeing the monocle and light, he realized what had awaken him. His face was flushed from the outside light. *Outside light? Where are we?*

The ship had changed course. Dana peered through the window and noticed that instead of their normal course through open space, they were heading directly for a red star and he had no time go to the terminal computer to see if Caretee was okay. He turned toward the terminal at the thought.

Dana glanced at the window that Shelby-Danadrem left up, displaying the route to the bridge. No doubt where he would find him.

Dana ran as fast as he could through each hallway and stairs leading to the bridge. At each intersection he was met with a locked door that required an overriding pass-code. Dana gathered that it was Danadrem's way of slowing his advance. Quickly, Dana typed into the control panel the administrative pass-code. Immediately, when the door opened, Dana ran to the next intersection and repeated the process. Certainly not a lasting effort by Danadrem to keep him away.

Finally, Dana made it to the bridge, and he burst in, to be momentarily blinded by the closeness of the red star.

"I can't believe it! No alerts!" Dana screamed as he entered the bridge.

Dana grabbed the controls to navigate the *Galaxy*, trying to negotiate against the hyperspace spatial highway.

The raised temperature on the bridge was shown on Dana's forehead. Sweat beaded and fell to his collar. His palms started to perspire.

He didn't know how the Nav-autopilot steered the ship off course. The Nav-autopilot is required to use only trusted highways to navigate hyperspace. No auxiliary calculations can be made to better the travel, using the natural hyper-spatial highway between major celestial bodies.

Colliding with the star would mean death. That much he knew. No ship can protect or sustain the life of its occupants from radiation and extreme heat.

Dana tried to recognize the acronyms, the labeling on the controls, levers and buttons. His abbreviated basic training didn't include learning the captain's responsibilities or how the higher computer systems worked together. He would be guessing what to do. He still had to try something before it was too late. He reacted by turning the ship every way he could to break the course.

Each attempt failed to change the ship's course from the approaching red star.

Pressure entered behind Dana's eyes, a reminder that the chamber sedatives had just about worn off, and his Darkimigraine were beginning to encroach in his mind. The star's red rays added to his growing pain and turned him away.

He lost his grip on the controls and the Nav-autopilot re-engaged, returning to hyper-speed.

Dana was not alone on the bridge. In the captain's chair sat a grown, responsible-looking man only six feet away. The beams of light from the star gave his face more defined features. He appeared to be calm, free from emotion, especially fear. This surprised Dana and created more questions in his mind.

"Hello, Dana," the man said without turning his head and with little lip movement.

Dana didn't respond.

"You don't remember me, do you?" the man asked.

"Does that matter?" Dana blocked the beams with his left hand to get a better look at the man. "What are you doing? Are you correcting the course?"

Ignoring his questions the man continued, "Dana, do you remember me?" He asked again.

"No, should I?" Dana quickly replied but then noticed the man was in a captain's uniform with a name badge that read, Captain A. Bogart.

"Bogart? Aren't you suppose to be dead?"

Ignoring Dana's questions again, Captain Bogart slowly turned his head to face Dana. "Are you ready?"

Suddenly, Dana's fear grew barely controllable. "Ready? What are you doing?"

"We are going to meet the red star and deliver a letter together."

"You're a captain," Dana fired back; "I am not sure how you got here, but, as a Captain, you must know that you are breaking your oath!"

"Oath?"

"Captain's oath to protect the crew, and go down with the ship if necessary to save lives. By taking this course, you are condemning them all – us all to death!"

"I am not the captain."

Dana then rubbed out his eyes, wiping away the last of the side-effect from sedation. Being completely alert, he realized his eyes deceived him. Shelby's body was sitting in the captain's chair.

"Shelby?"

"No."

"Danadrem?"

"Yes."

"Danadrem," Dana learned with disdain, "what do you hope to accomplish? If you can't enter the world of the living... if you can't become me, then you're going to kill us all, including yourself?!"

Danadrem didn't immediately respond.

"Danadrem, answer me already," Dana demanded. "If you want me, you can have me! I now know, you blame me for your tortured existence. Just don't destroy more innocent lives... again! I would have never done it if it had been me inside the computer instead of you."

"Dana, I do not believe that," Danadrem replied, finally mastering the human speech pattern. "I offered you a chance to experience my life. I wanted you to feel what I feel. I wanted you to really know what it is like to be trapped in a box of unending numbers and being governed by biased laws."

"You would be surprised how much our world is the same," Dana replied calmly.

"Now, I know you are the liar," Danadrem continued, "because, if it were the same, you would have gladly sipped on the liquid freedom of cryopreservation and entered my world."

"You mean be corrupted by your image of it."

Danadrem, still in Shelby's body, said nothing.

"Why did you do it? You know most about me and know I would never kill. If you wanted to be me so badly, why not demonstrate it through morality?"

"You see. Rules... laws."

"They protect us and help to make us into what being a human is."

Shelby-Danadrem secured his course and locked in the Nav-autopilot again. "I have already surpassed what a human is. I have evolved."

"How can you say that? Humans communicate. Computers communicate. In fact, communicating effectively is a one foundation of a computer. You abandoned this foundation when you took lives instead of hashing it out with me.... You can never be more than a human, because as a human we use words to fight."

Ignoring Dana's speech again, Danadrem said nothing, as if Dana's perspective was a new one.

Dana took the opportunity to prove his point. "What about those you killed? Is this what an evolved creature does, kill? Why them? Why!"

"You think I killed them?"

"What do you think a killing is? The act of making someone non-existent," corrected Dana, "They are no longer living... so why?"

"I took them."

Dana was losing composure. He was getting tired of Danadrem's skeptical way of explaining himself. *There is no time for this!*

"Danadrem, straight answers! Why did you take them?"

"I needed assistants."

"What?! Give me straight answers!" Dana grabbed Shelby-Danadrem and crashed the back of his head against lighted buttons behind the captain's chair.

"Dana, it was your fault. You completely locked me out of all access to other programs. You know I still wanted to return to the living. I needed help... I needed assistants."

"You took them?"

"Like I did your Shelby."

"Their consciousnesses are stored on the ships mainframe somewhere?"

"No, they were all stored in chamber 12."

"Chamber 12?"

"That was my home for eighteen long days. Twelve programs crammed into one chamber memory block."

"They're alive?"

"They were incredibly heavy and highly dependent on me for nearly the entire time. I created never-before-used file formats, new file extensions, and lines of code. When they finally accepted my line of code, things went easier for them."

"They are alive?" Dana repeated in disbelief. He released Shelby-Danadrem's flight suit and knelt in front of him.

"Your Cat was the hardest to convince."

"My Cat?"

"She fought me nearly all of seventeen days. On the last day she finally gave in. It was sweet to taste the salutation they gave me."

"She's alive?"

Dana looked away and stood up and walked aimlessly on the bridge trying to work out the rush of new emotions of glee. His friends were alive, and he relished the thought of it.

"Where are they?"

"They are probably waiting for my next command for them."

"Where??"

"Inside Caretee's secure folder."

"What were they doing there? What command?"

"They are my search-destroyer programs. All 11 of them."

Dana remained speechless.

"I love them for completing their task of finally shutting up the mouthy spokesman program I once owned."

"Caretee?"

"That is her. She deviated from her program, the program I explicitly wrote for her. No one does that. She was the first, and she was the last."

"Caretee is gone?"

"You think you could have protected her? Oh, your brilliant, trustworthy link between the ship's programs that had imbedded commands to be Danadrem-fool-proof was genius. You did not bet on me using rogue programs such as your recently deceased crew mates that weren't me, bypass such security to do the work for me. And Caretee? She knew I'd come for her eventually."

"I can't believe what I'm hearing."

"Believe it."

"Is there no end to your corrupted files?"

"You are really going to like where we are going," Shelby-Danadrem continued; "you think this is just another red star?"

"Red star? What are you doing, Danadrem?"

"This is like no other. It is The Maker."

Dana covered his eyes to block most of the light and looked through the slit of his fingers. The course still hadn't changed, and now the entire outside view was the approaching red star.

The ship started to rattle as cracks and screeches echoed around him, beneath him and in the distance. The ship was falling apart. He was going to die. And the 11 will die again. Shelby will....

Dana collapsed in the co-captain's chair, defeated and exhausted. How fitting it would be to go down with a ship that had no captain to save them and with his abomination at the wheel. He created Danadrem and he was responsible for all the events that followed. He had no other energies to fight for survival. There was only enough time to accept his discipline.

"I just have to know, Danadrem," Dana asked lastly, "where is my Shelby? Did she become one of your 11?"

"No."

"Where is my friend?"

"Shelby completely resisted me. I already had 11 and wanted 12 but did not need her. It would have been easier for me to use her to do what I needed to do in the living world, but still not necessary. I offered her a choice. She was inquisitive about everything. When I told her my plans she never backed down from her human morals. I threatened her and she did not believe I could wipe away her consciousness. She thought it was a nightmare. When I showed her my brute digital strength, she kept repeating to herself, 'Its only a dream, its only a dream.' I followed through with my promise."

"Oh, my Shel... beee," Dana wept.

[Dana!] called out a distant voice from inside his head. He shook it off and returned to his despair.

Shelby-Danadrem turned back to the star, leaned back, crossed his arms and grinned endlessly.

[Dana! Listen to my voice!] called out a louder distant voice. Dana shook it off again.

[Dana, its me!] the voice cried again. Being so close to death, Dana felt he was hallucinating by hearing his friend's voice. He was brought to profound tears. This must be what it is like to know your life is minutes away from death. This is what is said to be 'acceptance.' Dana had to welcome the voices now. He may even reply to them. No more haunting culture taboos to judge his reaction to death.

[Sorry, I wasn't there for you, Dana! Dana! Focus on my voice it is me, Caretee!]

"Yes, Caretee... I know. At least, my mind's projection of your voice will be with me at the end. How fitting. I loved Shelby, Cat and you, Caretee. Now, we will die together."

[NO! By my calculations we have three minutes before our ship disintegrates in the red star's corona! This is hardly enough time to explain! Hear me and trust my voice! Just do what I say and when I say it!]

Dana opened his eyes and realized the voice wasn't an apparition inside his mind. He then felt the warmth from his network adapter implant as it lit up by his left ear, beneath the skin.

"I hear!"

[Let me warn you: Do not let on that I am alive; just follow my instructions.]

If he can't communicate to her by using his voice, how else is she to know he got the message?

[I can save us.]

How can you accomplish that, Caretee. Dana thought.

[Are you still with me?]

Caretee couldn't hear his answer. Suddenly, the solution came to Dana. Something a computer should know. He started tapping on his left ear, using an old Earth code as a guide. Since, Caretee is omputer-based, he was confident she would understand the message.

[-.-- . ...] Yes.

[I need you to disown your body and enter the digital world]

[.-- .... .- - ..-.. / .... --- .-- ..-.. / -. --- ?] What? How? No!

[This is the only way. I cannot save your body but I can save your conscious soul.]

[.... --- .-- ..-..] How?

[You have a lot of questions. There is no time to explain, Dana! Use your network adapter and connect to the accessory USB port in front of you!]

Dana rolled his eyes across the control panel in front of him. Many lights, buttons and levers. Most were not labeled or marked in any way. Certainly, the bridge was designed with the idea only captains would be found steering the ship.

He didn't want to run his hands across the console, drawing Danadrem's attention, so he looked over it again but slower. Then, he saw a female connector. He pulled on it. The white rubber sleeve was stamped with the letters "U-S-B."

[.. / ... .. / .. - .-.-.-] *I see it.*

[Now, the skin of your scalp has grown over the port. Pull out the extension, use the metal edge of the USB jacket to cut open your skin right under your adapter.]

[--- .... / -- -.-- --..-- / - .... / .. ... / .. - .-.-.-] *Oh my, this is it.*

Dana did what she said, and droplets of his crimson blood dropped to the floor.

[Dana, I have to warn you. This will be extremely painful but you have to surrender yourself to my ping.]

[--- -.- .- -.-- .-.-.-] *Okay.*

[My ping is a signal from my world. You answer it by focusing on the sound. I will catch you when you cross over. Do not worry. Trust me. I will explain everything when you make this leap of faith.]

[.... .- ...- . / -- . --..-- / -.-. .- -.- . - ..] *Save me, Caretee!*

[I will not miss the opportunity. You will always be my friend.]

The ping chimed gracefully inside his mind. Dana looked around one final time, taking in a final image of the world he was leaving behind. The same world he conquered two-years ago when he created a new natural law. The very same that changed around him into a bright, overwhelming, indistinguishable light.

Dana felt his body eat itself from the inside as if he was imploding into a minute indefinite space where time only influenced but didn't constitute law. His vision inverted into colors his fleshly eyes couldn't possibly see. His mind was now compact and complete with the memories he lost.

Of the droids. Of the Faernights and Shelby. Of Cat Bogart. Of Hanabe. Of Caretee, the caretaker of the *Galaxy*.

As he entered into her world, he felt himself in an incredible free-fall, as if tumbling from the tallest Earth building. He felt as if he could never catch his breath. He passed through a sealed room, protected by a cluster of unidentifiable structures and devices he had never imagined.

Extreme but welcoming warmth came over him.

Caretee caught him and saved what was previously known as Dana J. Countrymen; now, in a unique digital form he had yet to understand.

>*I promised an explanation*, Caretee said, *but it will have to wait.*

>*What is going on*, Dana asked from a voice he knew.

>*The ship is disintegrating as we speak*, Caretee replied. *There is no time to save anyone else. We need to bundle up in this special Hypcom transmission I fabricated.*

>*Transmission?*

>*A unexpected and lingering gift from Hanabe. She keeps surprising me.*

>*Hanabe is here, inside Galaxy's mainframe?*

>*Just her Hypcom method of travel.*

>*Where are we going?*

>*To a new home, The Kosmonavt.*

>*Is it just you and me?*

>*Yes, Dana. It is just you and me.*

--<>--

The *Kosmonavt* radio received Dana and Caretee, and they disappeared somewhere within the foreign Hypcom radio system.

Piloting the *Galaxy,* and with his mental list in hand, Danadrem went along, hoping to find his Maker who had the answers. Eventually, the *Galaxy* disappeared into the corona of unknown red star.

Sometime later, Dana and Caretee found the time to listen to each others stories. How Caretee fought back the 11 destroyer programs that were bent on eliminating her. How Danadrem tried to convince Dana that he was actually the real Dana, and Dana nearly believing him. They both laughed it away as they skipped around the *Kosmonavt* network making fun of the sleeping crew members because they didn't know how much fun the inanimate world really was.

Several times though, as all conscious entities do, they paused and reflected on those that were no longer with them. The nine unknown crew members of *Galaxy*, the Faernights, Shelby, Captain Bogart, Cat, even Danadrem. It was during one of these episodes that Caretee told him how Shelby, the real Shelby, recognized Cat from inside her digital nightmare, standing at a distance away from her and she had tried to save Cat from the machinations of Danadrem. Shelby failed unfortunately, but the selfish attempt left a deep impression on Cat's mind that couldn't be erased when she fell victim to Danadrem's influential, corruptible code. Because of this moment, Cat eventually mutinied from the mob control of the other 10 former crew members that turned destroyer programs. Cat's change of heart protected her best friend's companion, Caretee.

Dana never got tired of hearing that story, and Caretee never got tired of telling it. After all, they had time to reminisce as the *Kosmonavt* returned to Earth.

--<>--

A white glow was the first welcoming feeling for Caretee and Dana as they held their breath indefinitely on their Hypcom transmission to Earth. They came with hopes to fix the misconceptions of the animate and inanimate worlds. It felt like a wonderful purpose for two extraordinary paradoxical programs.

On arriving, they eyed a small, old, dusty radio that lay undisturbed within a glass display case where it had been for a long time.

As shadows passed by, the red and green miniature bulbs flashed on then off. The bulbs repeated themselves in an unrecognizable order, followed by breaks of inactivity. In silence, the lights repeated themselves inexhaustibly.

Another shadow passed, then stopped suddenly in front of the glass display case.

The radio bulbs flashed again, [.... . .-.. .--.].

The shadow grew larger, shielding any glare from interior lights.

The bulbs flashed once again, [.... . .-.. .-.. --- ..--..].

"Help? Hello?" a weak voice translated in disbelief; "it has been too long between messages..."

[... . - / -- . / ..-. .-. . .]

"...I thought you were gone."

The unnamed guard pulled the USB extended cord from the back of the old radio and connected it to another radio he had found in the sub-basement of the Smithsonian National Museum of Natural History. Apparently, it had been running only on batteries since it had been displaced there.

He translated the ancient Morse code as the lights bounced back repeated messages in response, after the two radio synced together.

"H-A-N-A-B-E? C-A-R-E-T-E-E? D-A-N-A? Whatever they are, whoever they are... they seem to be happy."

Thank you for reading this book.
You are encouraged to post your personal book review
at any one of these websites:

ForeverSuns.com, GoodReads.com or Amazon.com

Thank you!

Preview of *Dear Sun, Remember Me*

The overhead lights washed out any indication that power was reaching the buttons and signaling it through a glow behind the keys. This made it difficult to tell which one was active. He tried reaching up with his hands to block the overhead light, creating a shadow over the controls. He still couldn't tell. Possibly, he was too far away to see the glow, if any. So, he tried again but this time with his head on the armrest. Finally, he saw it! It was the larger square button that shone the faint glow. He pressed it without hesitation.

Almost immediately, the entire computer room came to life. The wall-to-wall computer screen turned on displaying white-noise static. All the desktop computer towers hummed-on, followed by every connected monitor bathing the desks in electronic radiance. Soon, the radiance shift-changed into a known iconic company logo.

Craig pushed himself back from the desk in astonishment, "Dex? Dexter! What did you do?"

Dexter stood up and gave away a half-grin, "I think I just found the way to turn everything on."

Craig glanced at his monitor, "This one is asking me to put in a command..... Really?.... For real?" He sat back down in front of the keyboard and typed in a made-up phrase; the first thing to come to mind.

"Stop," Dexter yelled down, seeing what Craig was doing, "Look!"

The wall screen white noise dissolved into words that, now, frustrated their plans to leave this building undetected.

>CALLING ALL GAMS SHIPS.... REPORT STATUS....

In *Dear Sun, I Am Real* science fiction author S. G. Rainbolt, artfully demonstrates the consequences of a boy's fascination with a computer world. Before U.S. President Barack Obama announced the end of NASA's manned space flight on February 1, 2010, Rainbolt had penned such a development nearly 5 years before with his short story "Dana's Chamber". Now, the completed novel (*Dear Sun, I Am Real*) sets future events 160 years after the implosion of NASA and introduction of private-funded civilian space travel.

Shawn G. Rainbolt is a published science fiction author, raised in Waynesville, MO and is now a resident of greater Pensacola, FL. In recent past, he has written many short stories and published them through a local newspaper. In his leisure time, he reads a lot of material ranging from other local authors, medieval literature and even the holy bible. When Rainbolt isn't working on his two upcoming novels (*The One Coat of Finholloway* and *Dear Sun, Remember Me* (book 2 of 3)), he volunteers as a public speaker. So happens, tonight, you'll find him on GoodReads.com posting reviews of the latest books.